# *Dirty Hands*

A novel by

T.R. Braxton

MONTEBELLO BOOKS

2012 Edition

About the author:

T.R. Braxton is a native of Baltimore, Maryland. Dirty Hands is his first published novel. Braxton is proud of the tireless work he has put into writing and publishing this thrilling novel. His talent is expansive as future novels delve into horror and the supernatural.

Author website: www.trbraxton.com

What others are saying about Dirty Hands:

"Dirty Hands will give you a ride you'll never forget. I'm still thinking about it, and that is exactly what an author is supposed to make a reader do."

M.L. St. Sure, author of Evensong.

"It's a rare book that focuses on the "bad guys," building up sympathy for or, at least, understanding of their actions. Author T. R. Braxton does this well."

Clayton Bye, reviews.thedeepening.com

"Braxton is a master of street slang and inner-city vernacular. His three main characters speak with a gritty yet fluid street lingo that almost becomes its own dialect."

Mark McGinty, theboogle.wordpress.com

This book is dedicated to Jack Brax, also known as Besowitz Bashoyntin, my best friend, strongest supporter, and truest critic. Thank you for always being there for me.

# Dirty Hands

# Chapter One

I

A diminutive young woman lay sprawled at Terrell Hawkins's feet. Her ample bosom remained still, betraying no breath.

"She's dead." Terrell's cousin Brock confirmed Terrell's fears, speaking in a choked voice from the tiled bathroom floor.

A ring of blood highlighted the hair at the crown of the young woman's skull. Her head collapsed to one side when Terrell pressed his middle and index fingers against her neck. Neither her neck nor her wrist revealed a pulse.

"I told you… she's dead," Brock moaned. He sounded as if he were on the verge of tears.

Terrell's first thought was that if he had kept a low profile while Monet was visiting her sick mother in Virginia Beach, this horrible situation couldn't have occurred. Instead, he agreed to let Brock and their friend Shawntae bring some random sluts to his apartment in northeast Baltimore. If he had said no or at least not participated in the debauchery that ensued, there wouldn't be a dead girl in his bathroom. His mind returned to earlier that night, recalling the events that led him into a drunken, post-coital slumber as the girl at his feet lost her life.

II

Red plastic cups and bottles of alcohol in various states of depletion littered the floor of Terrell's living room. Cigar guts and ashes rested in two paper bowls that served as makeshift ashtrays.

One a.m. approached as a malevolent sky threatened the early June night. Plied with alcohol and marijuana, Tia and Tiffany Jenkins danced like strippers in training as Brock and Shawntae leered at them from Terrell's couch.

Their friend Heloise sucked her teeth. "They always act so raunchy," she said, seated next to Terrell on his loveseat, close enough for her skirted thigh to brush his leg.

He leaned toward her, struggling to hear over the blaring stereo. "What did you say?"

"I said they act so raunchy!" Heloise's throaty voice was honey in Terrell's ear. Her pleasant smell held echoes of fruit. Her breasts were full, her legs long and lean.

Now that he'd been drinking, Terrell lost sight of his assigned role for the evening. He was supposed to play polite host to Heloise, giving Brock and Shawntae time and space to get the two sisters into bed. Though he hadn't had one pull of marijuana, Heloise's stunning attractiveness combined with the mind numbing effects of alcohol to push Monet far from his mind.

Terrell smiled. "Yeah," he said. "I like quiet girls- like you."

Heloise giggled. "I like you, too." She was no more sober than Terrell was.

The sisters continued their antics, teasing their audience by grinding against each other.

Riled up by the lurid dancing, Shawntae placed a tree like arm around Tiffany's tiny waist, pulling her tight against him. "Come on, girl," he said, pressing his crotch against her rear end. "I got somethin' betta for you to grind on."

Terrell smiled as Shawntae and his soon to be notch on the belt walked toward Malik's bedroom. Malik had left Baltimore for Brooklyn the day after Morrison University's spring semester ended. His uncle had lined up a good summer job for him there. It had been agreed upon that whoever had the good fortune of putting some mileage on Malik's bed springs would be responsible for straightening his quarters afterward. Terrell felt no doubt that Shawntae would clean up with a huge grin plastered on his face.

Moments later, Heloise asked to see Terrell's bedroom. He knew that he should brush her off, but he was far too drunk and she was far too sexy to refuse. He regarded her statuesque frame as they entered. Two-inch pumps brought her almost even with his 6-1 height.

They hadn't been on Terrell's bed for ten minutes before Heloise confessed that the weed and alcohol had made her feel horny. She asked if Terrell felt as horny as she did.

"What's it look like?" he slurred, whipping Terrell Junior out. Monet cast not even a shadow of a thought in his drunken, lustful mind.

Heloise giggled, brushing his little friend with her left hand.

"Whatchu want me to do wit' that?"

"You're a big girl. I don't think you need instructions."

After Heloise finished treating his trouser snake like the world's sweetest lollipop, Terrell plowed her in various positions. He paused once when he heard a crashing noise.

He looked down at Heloise. "You hear that?"

"Who gives a fuck?" she said, coiling her legs around the small of his back. "Finish fuckin' me. You were doing so good."

Terrell managed another dozen pleasurable thrusts or so before spilling his load into the condom he wore. He and Heloise then collapsed into drunken and satisfied slumber.

They remained in that state until Brock crept into the room and shook Terrell awake.

III

Terrell's awakening senses failed to make out what his cousin was saying. "Wh-uuut?" he groaned.

"Shh!" Brock placed a trembling finger over his own trembling lips. "Git up. I gotta show you something."

Drunken grogginess did not stop Terrell from recognizing the shakiness in his cousin's voice. He rose from the bed, taking care not to awaken Heloise.

The earlier foreboding sky had given way to a tremendous rainstorm as Terrell slept. Flashes of lightning and crackling thunder announced heaven's fury.

Terrell slipped his boxers back on and closed the bedroom door behind him, becoming aware of the eerie silence that permeated his apartment.

Brock's eyes were the size of saucers. His body leaked sweat.

"What's wrong, cuz?" Terrell whispered.

"I fucked up, man," Brock spoke in an anguished moan. "I really fucked up."

"What are you talkin' about?"

Brock motioned for Terrell to follow him. They walked into the bathroom. Tia lay still there, across the naked floor tiles.

Having confirmed the girl's death, Terrell hauled his much smaller cousin to his feet. He stared into Brock's distraught eyes. "Tell me how this happened."

IV

Brock didn't need video footage to know what was happening in the bedrooms. He figured that it was time for him and Tia to get down to the business of slapping bellies as well.

Tia had different ideas about how matters should proceed. Instead of rushing to what Brock felt was the inevitable conclusion; she took great pleasure in teasing him, making him wait.

She played peek-a-boo, exposing her breasts before tucking them away again. She rubbed Brock's crotch through his jean shorts, then backed away, laughing. Just when he'd had enough of her antics, she unzipped his shorts and pulled them below his knees.

Her full lips unfurled into a devil's smile as she kneeled in front of the couch and stared up at him. "Don't nut while I'm doin' this, because I want you to fuck me real good."

A few pleasurable minutes later, someone knocked on the door. Brock ignored it at first, but the knocking persisted.

Tia urged him not to answer.

"I have to," he explained, rising to his feet and fixing his clothes. "It might be somethin' serious."

Seated on the couch once more, Tia folded her arms in a displeased pose. "What could be more serious than what I was jus' doin'?"

Brock ignored Tia and looked through the people to see Terrell's upstairs neighbor. Brock didn't remember the man's name. He thought of him as the chubby dude who worked for Baltimore Gas and Electric.

The man said that his wife had henpecked him into coming downstairs and asking that they turn the music down. Brock apologized for the disturbance and agreed to do as asked.

After carrying out the request, Brock sidled back over to Tia. He felt surprised to find her face flushed with anger. He wondered if he should leave well enough alone before thinking of the world class oral skills she had just demonstrated. He decided that he had to see what else she could do.

"Come on, sexy." Brock leaned over her. "Le's pick up where we left off."

"Fuck that!" she hissed. "Didn't I ask you not to answer the door?"

Brock's eyes expanded like rising yeast. "How you gon' be mad about that? I had to git it. Somethin' serious could have been goin' on. People don't jus' knock on their neighbor's doors in the middle of the night for no reason."

"Somethin' serious was goin' on." Tia's eyes blazed in anger. "I was breakin' you off. Nigga, this shit is exclusive. Not everybody gits to sample this."

Brock thought of her reputation and laughed so hard that he rolled into the floor.

“I don’t see nothin’ funny!” Tia bellowed.

Brock knew that he was provoking her, but he just couldn't stop laughing.

“I don’t know why I bother messin’ wit’ these bullshit dudes,” she grumbled, her sand colored face turning a harsh crimson.

“Bullshit?” Brock bellowed, his laughter changing to hostility in an instant. “Who the fuck you callin’ bullshit? You fuckin’ whore!”

“Who the fuck you callin’ a whore?” Tia hissed. Her head looked set to fly from her shoulders.

Brock didn’t miss a beat in upping the ante. “I’m callin’ you a whore. Tha’s what the fuck you are!”

Tia launched herself at him. Brock warded off a flurry of blows before pushing her down on the couch. He pinned his weight against her and held her wrists. “Yo… are you fuckin’ crazy or somethin’?”

“Git the fuck off me!” Tia's teeth gnashed as she screeched. She bucked and twisted like a wild mare trying to throw an unwelcome rider.

Brock fell silent as he restrained her. Corded veins bulged in her slender arms and neck as she continued to thrash about. Brock’s own muscles strained as he waited for her to tire.

“Are you calm?” Brock asked in a weary voice when her struggles abated.

Tia answered in a near whisper. “Yes. Now git off me.”

"If I git off you are you gon' come at me again?"

"No."

"You swear?"

"I swear."

"I mean it. I don't want no more of this. We ain't sposed to be fightin' in here. That don't make no kinda sense, baby girl."

Tia's voice softened. "I know. I swear I won't try to fight you anymore, Brock."

Brock backed away. Malice filled Tia's eyes as she swung her fisted right hand at him. Brock's instincts took over, causing him to dodge the blow and circle behind her. As she pivoted to renew her assault, he grabbed her around the waist and hoisted her from the floor.

As the diminutive fury struggled to get free, Brock used one arm to carry her toward the bathroom and the other to ward off more blows.

"Oh, you a hothid," he teased. "Huh? I'm a hothid, too. I tell you what- we both gon' cool down in the shower."

Tia screeched. "Git the fuck offa me!"

As they struggled into the bathroom, Tia grabbed Brock's free arm and chomped on his wrist. He dropped her as he howled, "You crazy bitch!"

Tia regained her balance and rushed him again.

Brock thrust his arms outward, catching his assailant flush in the chest with both palms. Her feet lifted from the floor as her small body flew backward. For the split second that she was airborne, she looked like a tailback on the wrong end of a collision with Ray Lewis. A ripping sound was joined by six simultaneous pings as the cheap shower curtain tore free from the bar it hung from and the plastic rings that had held it in place popped like popcorn kernels. Tia's momentum carried the curtain with her, but it did nothing to stop her head from caroming off the inside lip of the bathtub. A sickening thud resounded as her head rebounded upward before settling into a canted position against the lowest of the wall tiles that overlooked the tub. Her splayed feet hung over the edge of the bathtub as her limp arms dangled like those of a rag doll. A dot of blood marred the spot where her head had struck.

Brock composed himself after a long stillness, taking great care in lifting Tia from the tub. The gruesome sight of her dented skull and ruined neck forced him to accept the reality of her death. He treated her broken form like a precious piece of china as he laid her on the bathroom floor.

"So that's how it happened." Brock slumped against the towel rack, having finished his horrid account. "I can't believe this shit is real."

"Neither can I," Terrell said, his lips trembling.

They both fell still and silent, remaining that way until Shawntae sauntered into the bathroom. "Shit, shorty got some good pussy," he chuckled, drawing closer.

V

The sight of Tia's limp body wiped the satisfied grin off Shawntae's face. An expression of sheer shock replaced it.

"Oh, shit. Oh shit, man!" he gasped, his wide frame clad only in boxer shorts. "How the fuck did this happen?

A stream of tears flowed down Brock's face as he answered. "I killed her, Tae. It was an accident, but I killed her. I fuckin' killed her."

"What the fuck are we gonna do?" Terrell asked as he pulled the door close.

Footfalls approached from the hall before any of them could answer. They cringed at the sound of Tiffany's voice outside the bathroom door.

"Tae?" She called. "Where you at? You in the bathroom? Can I come in? I need to go!"

Tae stammered his answer. "H-hold on, baby."

"Hurry up!" she said. "I'ma check on Tia. I hope she feelin' right like I am. Iss been a while since I had some good lovin' like that. I'm gon' need some more of that, big man."

Terror gripped Terrell and Shawntae as Brock edged toward catatonia.

Seconds later, Tiffany yelled, "Hey! Where's my sista?"

Shawntae stepped into the hall in a vain attempt to keep her from the bathroom, but she barged right past him.

"I don't like this sh…Omigod!" she gasped, "Tia! Omigod!"

She fell to her sibling's side, trying in vain to revive her.

"How the fuck did this happen?" she screeched, her eyes and voice frantic. "She ain't breathin'! Why ain't she breathin?"

After receiving no answer, Tiffany fell silent. All traces of emotion deserted her countenance as she walked trance-like from the bathroom.

"I know she'll be alright," she murmured. "She'll be alright. This is just a mistake. Iss all a mistake. We have to call the police. We have to call an ambulance."

Terrell and Shawntae shadowed the distraught girl as she reached for the phone that was mounted in Terrell's kitchenette. Shawntae grabbed her from behind, covering her mouth with one meaty hand.

"I'm sorry, Tiffany," he sighed. "We can't call nobody."

Tiffany grabbed his large mitt with her own small, delicate hands and bit down, throwing her neck into the effort. She clamped down, savaging him like a rabid pit bull.

"Argh. Argh!" Shawntae wailed in pain.

"Fuck you!" Tiffany screeched as Shawntae wrenched free. Drops of crimson leaked from his hand, landing on the tiled floor of the kitchenette.

"Fuck!" He screamed, holding his offended appendage. Tiffany scrambled to grab one of the discarded alcohol bottles, breaking it against the dining table that sat adjacent to the kitchenette. An entranced Brock emerged from the bathroom as Tiffany pointed the jagged end at Shawntae.

"You muthafuckas killed my little sista and now I'm gon' kill all of y'all!"

Shawntae pleaded, holding both hands out in front of him. Blood continued to escape his wound. "Easy, Tiffany. It ain't gotta be like that."

Terrell stepped in front of his friend, with no clear plan in mind. He only knew that he didn't want Shawntae to get hurt again.

Hatred painted Tiffany's eyes as she feinted at Terrell with her makeshift weapon. Terrell realized just how much danger he was in when she didn't mount a wild charge. She intended to strike with accuracy.

Brock exploded into the scene, flying at Tiffany as if shot from a cannon. He twisted his whole body into a right cross, sending the petite girl crumpling into the living room carpet. Instead of pausing to check out his handiwork, he marched into Terrell's bedroom. Terrell heard the unmistakable sound of fist striking flesh.

"What'd you do?" Shawntae asked, still nursing his ravaged hand as Brock returned.

"I knocked the otha chick out, too," Brock answered. "What the fuck were y'all gon' do?" He rubbed the knuckles of his right hand. "Let that bitch cut you up? Let those chicks keep makin' noise until somebody called the cops?"

He walked over to the couch and sat down.

"Now what?" Shawntae asked, looking down at Tiffany.

"We gotta convince these girls not to talk about this," Terrell answered.

Shawntae looked at him with disdain. "The fuck are you- crazy? That's her sister dead in the bathroom 'n' shorty back there's her homegirl." He pronounced dead as *did.* "How the fuck we gon' keep these bitches from talkin'?"

Terrell shrugged. "There's gotta be a way. I mean… we could just explain to them what happened. It was an accident. Maybe they'll understand."

"You must have bumped your head harder than that chick in the bathroom," Shawntae snapped, pronouncing head as *hid*. "They just sposed to accept that Brock killed shorty's sista 'n' we tryna' cover it up – 'n' tha's s'posed to be alright wit' them? Naw, Terrell. We gotta find some other way to keep them quiet."

"There's only one way to keep this quiet." Brock's voice was devoid of emotion. "Y'all know that."

"Man, don't talk stupid," Terrell broke the long silence that followed. "We are not murderers! This shit started out as an accident, but what you're talkin' about is takin' it to another level."

"It ain't stupid, Terrell. Iss real. What the fuck could we tell the cops? That I accidentally killed Tia while defendin' myself and then I knocked out the other two to protect y'all? Would they believe that shit?"

"Iss the truth, Brock," Shawntae said. "We didn't mean to hurt that girl 'n' we didn't mean for any of this to happen."

"Yeah?" Brock said, standing and making wild gesticulations. "Well iss also true that shorty over there is only 17 years old 'n' the other chicks are only 18. Plus none of us are 21 yet so, we ain't legal to buy alcohol but we're all drunk as skunks 'n' we got weed up in here- and we're three niggas 'n' the mayor's on some shit - stressin' bein' tough on crime. That ain't a good position to start from wit' the cops."

"So your idea is better than that?" Terrell argued. "You've killed one girl by accident- now you wanna go ahead and murder the other two? Man, one manslaughter charge is a lot better than three murder charges."

“You say that shit like manslaughter is a misdemeanor,” Brock countered. “I could git ten years for that shit alone. You know I already got assault charges on my record. ‘N’ you know they gon’ stick us wit’ them otha lil’ bullshit charges cuz we black.”

Brock paused for a moment. “Well, fuck that shit!” he bellowed. “I don’t wanna go to jail, period. ‘N’ if you think y’all wouldn’t git no time behind it, you fuckin’ crazy.”

“Man, I don’t give a fuck what you say about it,” Terrell said, a sneer on his face. “That shit ain’t happenin’.”

“It has to happen,” Shawntae spoke with grave resignation as he placed his right hand on Terrell’s shoulder.

Terrell scowled as he pushed the appendage away. “I can’t believe you agree with this shit, Tae!”

“Yo, T- if we don’t do this shit, our lives are ruined. You wanna have to git your college degree in jail? You think it’ll matter how smart you are when you gotta cop to some shit like this on job applications? Even if you don’t go to jail - you think Monet will still be down witchu after she finds out about this shit? You fucked that chick back there-didn’t you? You think any of our families will look at us the same if this comes out? They’ll be ashamed of us, man.”

“Fuck shame!” Terrell hissed. “That ain’t a consideration for me. I’m not tryna be involved in murder because I know it’s wrong! I know it's wrong and we could never atone for something like that.”

"What do you say, Brock?" Shawntae acted as if he hadn't heard a word Terrell said.

"You already know what I say."

Shawntae nodded, turning back to Terrell. "I'm sorry, man. But we're doin' it wit' or wit'out you."

Brock started toward Terrell's bedroom, where he looked down on Heloise. She started to stir, but fell still again when he punched her on the side of her head.

"What the fuck, man?" Terrell cried, having followed his cousin in. He moved in front of Heloise's unconscious form. Brock shrugged, holding his palms out as if to say he had no other choice.

"I'm not gonna let y'all do this," Terrell's said, his voice quavering.

Brock returned to where Tiffany lay. He pointed down at her. "Did she move any?"

"Nope," Tae answered, running water from the kitchenette sink over his wound. "You still got that first aid kid your mother gave you?" he asked Terrell.

Terrell removed the requested item from under the bathroom sink, foraging through it for a roll of gauze. "Never thought I'd need this shit, definitely not for anything like this," he said, handing the gauze to Tae. The big man used a good portion of it to cover his bleeding hand.

"I'm not gon' let y'all do this," Terrell repeated.

Shawntae removed the cordless telephone from its base and handed it to Terrell. As he did that, Brock returned to Terrell's bedroom. He emerged holding a pillow, awaiting the outcome of the ensuing contest of wills between his dearest cousin and his closest friend.

"Then go hid 'n' call the police," Shawntae said. "Go on. Call the police and send your own cous- fuck that, your brova to jail for a long time. We're all like brovas- or have you forgotten? Grew up within two blocks of each other. Ran around in the same East Baltimore streets- went to the same elementary and middle schools. Always been there for each other- through all kinds of shit. We alway*s* been there for each other. You tellin' me we not gon' be there for each other now? Then go hid. Go hid 'n' call the police - if you kin live wit' that."

Shawntae continued when Terrell offered no response. "Kin you live with that? Sendin' us all to jail?" 'N' for what? Some triflin' ass bitches? Them trashy bitches didn't even give a fuck about themselves. You really wanna throw our lives away on them?"

Terrell slumped into a chair at his humble dining table. The telephone slipped from his hand, coming to rest on the tabletop as noticed Tiffany starting to stir.

"No, I don't," he sighed, thinking of the girls with a mixture of sadness and disdain. "I don't wanna throw our lives away on them."

Salty tears slid down Terrell's face as Brock first smothered Tiffany, then Heloise with the pillow. The entire world faded away, leaving only Brock's ragged breathing and the lifeless eyes of the slain girls.

# Chapter Two

I

A rain slicker protected Terrell against the raging storm. Brock and Shawntae wore oversized hooded sweatshirts they had taken from Terrell's closet. The malevolent weather was the least of their worries. They thought that it might even work to their advantage.

They figured that only someone desperate or crazy would be out and about at such a late hour, during such terrible conditions. Since Baltimore had no shortage of either, they scanned the windows that overlooked the courtyard from the upper floors of the apartment complex. Not a single light shined.

Minutes earlier, the trio finished a thorough cleaning of Tia's blood from the tub and Shawntae's blood from the kitchenette floor. While doing so, they came to an agreement on how to dispose of the bodies. Once they were confident that no eyes were on them, they wrapped the diminutive bodies of the sisters into some spare sheets and stuffed them into the massive trunk of Brock's old Cutlass Supreme. Once that was done, Shawntae and Terrell returned to the apartment. Brock cranked the car's defroster all the way up as the others forced Heloise's body into the hall closet.

Terrell froze in place for a few seconds after that deed. "Come on, man," Shawntae said, tugging on his arm. They filled their hands with large black trash bags before heading back to the car. Brock navigated the storm with his high beams glaring, windshield wipers beating against the pounding water.

After several tense miles and a number of turns, Brock pulled the Cutlass into an alley harsh with darkness. He shifted the car into park and told his accomplices that he would be right back.

Shawntae sat mute in the passenger seat. Terrell was just as silent behind him. Brock climbed over his grandmother's backyard fence and approached the tool shed.

Brock had told Terrell and Shawntae a million times that his strung out Uncle Ramon kept a bunch of tools and supplies in the small wooden structure. The man was a truly skillful landscaper, although he only worked enough to support his substance abuse. He returned to the car with a large hatchet.

II

The Cutlass rested along the curve that ran parallel to a stretch of Herring Run Park's two mile length. Upon exiting the vehicle, the three young men scanned the immaculate row houses across the street, just above the Belair Road side of Chesterfield Avenue.

Once they felt satisfied that the neighborhood was as still as Terrell's apartment complex had been, Terrell, Brock, and Shawntae unloaded their macabre cargo. Shawntae hoisted one of the sheet wrapped bodies over a wide shoulder while Terrell and Brock teamed to carry the other. They trudged down a sloping hill before crossing the bike path that bisected it. A woody area extended along the bike path's opposite side. They soldiered through a grove of trees before terminating their trip at the edge of a roiling stream.

After they placed the bodies along the bank, Shawntae returned to the car and retrieved the trash bags. He stood lookout at the edge of the trees while Brock took the hatchet to what was left of Tia. The dull blade caught each time that it found her flesh, forcing him to wrench it free. Bone and tissue sprayed each time that he did so.

Terrell soon lost his cookies, spewing vomit as if a damn had burst open. Brock soldiered on until Tia was hacked into small pieces. He then dropped the hatchet and sent forth his own spew.

When he was done heaving the contents of his stomach, Brock looked at Terrell. He wiped spittle from his mouth and said, "I don't think I kin do the next one. My arms are too tired."

Terrell took a number of deep breaths, trying to still his inner turmoil enough to complete the grisly task at hand. He grasped the hatchet without speaking and proceeded to do the most horrible thing he'd ever done.

III

Lake Montebello was the next stop of the flash flood driving tour. Even during a world class rainstorm, the man-made marvel was less than a ten minute drive from the area where the girl's bodies had been dismembered. It stood less than a hundred yards away from the P.A.L. Center where Terrell worked.

The lake measured more than a mile in circumference. Dark metal fencing and short concrete walls bordered its' exterior. Its' shore sat low over the neat shrubs growing just beneath the fencing. The asphalt trail which mimicked the shape of the lake served as a hotspot for local fitness enthusiasts. The concrete walls blocked what had once been a west-bound driving lane, serving as a protection for said enthusiasts. The popular recreational area was just as deserted as the rest of the trio's stops had been during this ugly night.

Upon reaching their destination, the conspirators heaved the dead girls' dismembered and bagged body parts as far into the lake as possible. They took the extra caution of weighing each bagged appendage down with large rocks taken from Herring Run Stream.

The storm continued to rage during the return trip to Terrell's apartment. The streetlights slept, indicating a power outage. Terrell assumed that everyone else in his complex slumbered through it. His wristwatch told him that it was nearly 4 a.m.

He and the others rushed Heloise's much larger corpse into a huge comforter, transporting her to Herring Run Stream as they had the others. This time, Shawntae did the honors of dismemberment. Just as his accomplices had, he vomited everything himself empty when the grisly task was done.

Heloise's dismembered body parts were stuffed into several large garbage bags, just as the ill fated sisters' had been. Heavy rocks were again added before the bags were tied shut. Heloise's apportioned remains soon joined those of her murdered friends at the bottom of Lake Montebello.

A flashlight lit the way as Brock and Shawntae helped Terrell clean up the remaining wreckage in his apartment. They bagged up the alcohol and marijuana refuse. They cleaned every inch of the bathtub and its' ceramic tiled walls with ammonia, braving the eye watering stench.

"As hard as that chick must've hit, there ain't so much as a dent in that tub," Shawntae observed as he scrubbed away with his intact left hand.

"Yeah," Terrell agreed. "Must be really good craftsmanship."

"Maybe if it wasn't, that little chick might've lived."

Brock looked at the ruined showered curtain, which was now balled up next to the toilet. "You'll have to git a new shower curtain."

"I got two more of them in the linen closet. Gifts from Monet. You know she be tryna keep this place halfway decent."

Brock chuckled as he continued to wipe the outer edge of the tub. "It's a good thing she does. Otherwise, this place'd always look like a shithole."

They finished the bathroom before tackling the kitchenette again. They scrubbed and mopped every centimeter of it, behaving as if their lives depended on its spiffiness. Satisfied that the tiles were spotless, they all kneeled and searched the carpet in the living room/dining area, losing no time in disposing of the few hairs they found.

"I don't know how I'll ever take a shower in there again," Terrell said, holding an outstretched arm toward the bathroom.

"Sooner or later, you'll have to," Brock responded. He promised to get rid of the sheets and comforter they'd used. He and Shawntae left after sharing a few insubstantial parting words. Nothing they said referenced the terrible things that had just happened.

Terrell removed his wet garments and put on some raggedy basketball shorts. He scoured his kitchen cabinets for alcohol, finding a half-pint of

Crown Royal and a miniature bottle of Bacardi Rum. He managed to drink himself into oblivion by the time the sun rose.

IV

Terrell woke from his stupor with a pounding headache. Stark fear seized him, trapping him in its clutches. His heart pounded as he searched his living room for blood or hair, finding neither. That didn't stop him from visualizing a terrible CSI scenario. He imagined a forensic specialist spraying some type of chemical in his apartment, revealing glowing traces of incriminating blood and DNA.

He scrubbed his bathroom floor, sink, and toilet as if he suffered from OCD. His already sore arms felt a hundred times worse by the time he finished. Forehead beaded with sweat, he plopped down on the couch and cried.

Try as he might, he couldn't stop thinking about what happened. Three girls had been murdered in his apartment, by his cousin.

Terrell had done nothing to stop it and had even helped dispose of the bodies. It didn't take a rocket scientist to figure out that his life was over. Again he thought that if he had only kept his dick in his pants, things would have been different. Sure, there was no way to anticipate what happened, but if he had been true to Monet, he would have never been in the situation to begin with.

What was he supposed to do, though? Sit around knitting all weekend? He was a red-blooded, twenty year old American male. *Naw*, he admitted to himself. *That's no excuse. I shouldn't have fucked that girl. Flirting is one thing, but I shouldn't have fucked her. I should have just stayed to myself all weekend, beat my meat if I got horny. Fuck! If I hadn't gotten so fucking drunk, things wouldn't have gone so far.*

Terrell's mind flooded with visions of the girl's dead bodies lying on the embankment, of the dull hatchet rending them into human butcher's meat. He had swung the hatchet into Tiffany's flesh himself. He had done it again and again.

It hadn't been necessary for Heloise and Tiffany to die. He should have done something instead of allowing Tae to talk him into going along with it. But what could he have done? How could those girls be saved without someone going to jail? He knew that the thing with Tia was an accident. He also knew why Brock had murdered the others and why Tae had convinced him to allow it. His hands were just as dirty as the others' because he had submitted himself to Tae's logic.

Tae had asked Terrell if he wanted to throw his life away on those girls. Terrell had answered no. Now he wondered if his life was even worth anything after what he'd allowed to happen. His conscience continued torturing him until he decided to drink himself asleep again. He disregarded his queasy stomach and pounding head as he scoured his kitchen cabinet for more alcohol. Frustrated at not finding any, he hurled the empty Crown Royal bottle against his living room wall. It shattered into tiny shards.

Terrell left the wreckage in the floor and put on a full set of clothes. He went through the motions of washing his face, not caring that he looked like the living dead. His only concern was getting shit-faced, although his face looked pretty shitty already. He chuckled at that thought. Moments later, he sat out to trudge the five block distance to the Cedonia Inn. The gray rectangular structure was the only liquor store open on Sunday for miles. A line stretched out the door.

Terrell battled the effects of his previous binge, managing to steady himself until he reached the counter. He ordered a pint of Bacardi Gold and a 40 ounce Budweiser through the safety glass that separated the merchants from customers and would be robbers.

The sallow-faced cashier's brows rose as he drank in Terrell's ghastly appearance. "Are you sure you need anything to drink right now? You don't look so good."

"Just git me what I asked for," Terrell growled.

"Alright," the cashier said; a sheepish smile on his face. "Just don't hurt nobody."

Terrell forced a smile of his own. "I wouldn't hurt a fly."

Terrell obtained the requested alcohol along with his change, then trudged back to his apartment. He decided not to be completely self-destructive, drinking two glasses of water and forcing down a peanut butter and jelly sandwich before medicating himself back into oblivion.

V

It was past 3 a.m. the next morning when Terrell's stomach rebelled against its' mistreatment and began expelling the poison he had inundated it with. Sweat cascaded down his body as he prayed to the porcelain god. His stomach heaved again and again, until drained of contents. Exhausted, he lay on the rug in front of the toilet.

When he was able to stand, Terrell inspected his appearance in the bathroom mirror, trying not to think about the fact that a girl had died in this very room. His bloodshot eyes beheld his sickly pallor, scruffy facial hair, and short, unkempt afro. “I look like shit,” he said, chuckling without humor. He didn’t bother to clean himself up.

He did decide to get some nutrients into his body posthaste. His grand choices were Oodles of Noodles or hot dogs. He boiled two packs of the noodles, opting not to add the sodium blasted sauce to it. After draining the noodles of water, he mixed in some ketchup and hot sauce. He wolfed it all down prior to chasing the meal with two glasses of orange juice.

He felt his body crawl along the road to recovery. Although he wasn’t due at the PAL Center until noon, he felt too wired to go back to sleep. He played video games in an attempt to keep the demons at bay. The moving sprites of the Playstation 2 provided just enough distraction to keep him from having a panic attack.

Thumbs sore from repetitive pounding of the controller, Terrell glanced at his watch and discovered that time had rushed forward to nearly 10 a.m. He set the controller down and cleaned up the glass from the broken bottle. He noticed the red light that flashed on his phone to indicate that he had voice mail. He punched in the password and checked his messages.

There were several messages from Monet, which he deleted as soon as her cell phone was identified as the incoming number. He could not bear to even hear a recording of her voice in his present state. A message from his mother received the same treatment.

Terrell went into the bathroom and hung one of the shower curtains that Monet had given him. Knowing that he had to be presentable for work provided enough motivation for him to take a proper shower. He yelped his favorite rap lyrics as he did so, using the activity to beat back thoughts of how Tia had met her death in the very chamber that he now used to clean himself.

Terrell had never felt so grateful for the privilege of reporting to the Montebello Community Police Athletic League Center. As he exited the bus and approached the entrance, he tried not to think about the fact that he and his friends had pitched human remains into the lake a short distance away. Once inside, he greeted Officer Smith, who oversaw the center for the Baltimore City Police Department. As always, the well-muscled, square jawed, spike haired blond welcomed him with a firm handshake.

"Wassup, T?" he asked, smiling.

"Nothing much, Smitty," Terrell answered. "Did a little bit too much partying last night."

"You look it," the cop said, sizing him up. "I remember those days. You alright to work?"

"Yeah, man. I'm cool. I slept it off."

Officer Smith surprised Terrell by smelling him.

"Yeah. You're good," he whispered, not wanting any kids to hear him. "You weren't dumb enough to come here smelling of booze."

Terrell laughed. "Come on, Smitty. I would never disrespect like that."

Officer Smith shrugged. "You can't blame a white boy for checkin'."

Terrell threw himself into working with the kids after passing inspection. As always, they were happy to see him. He tried not to have a free moment, dreading being left alone with his terrible thoughts.

Later that afternoon, Terrell found himself engaged in a fierce game of dodge ball. The version of dodge ball that was played at the Center began with a bunch of kids gathered in the center of the basketball court. Two enders lined up at opposite ends of the group. The enders then took turns throwing kids out until they were down to one player.

If the last player avoided ten consecutive throws, they won the game and earned the privilege of being an ender for the next contest. They also had the privilege of choosing their partner.

Terrell treated dodge ball like a competitive sport. No child had ever won a game while he was an ender. Most of the kids loved playing with him because he never took it easy on them.

This day was no different. The game started off with about 20 kids in the middle. Terrell used every trick in his arsenal to whittle their ranks, playing the vinyl ball like a shortstop, charging in to field errant tosses and making accurate throws on the run. Even the fact that his partner Justina (another tutor/mentor) threw the ball as if the kids were made of porcelain couldn't save them from him.

After about ten minutes of spirited play, a ten-year old waterbug named Sammy was the only kid remaining.  Sammy was always a tough out and as the last player, he had all the space he could want in dodging throws. He avoided Terrell and Justina's first seven attempts with easy grace and quickness. He also drew attention to himself by yelling out the number of each missed throw. By the time the contest was down to the last three throws, the entire populace of the Center had become a raucous audience.

"Could this be the day?" Officer Smith yelled, stoking the enthusiastic atmosphere. "Could this be the day that the great Terrell finally loses?"

A cacophony of cheers erupted from the children alongside the court. Terrell wore a confident smile as he gathered an errant throw from Justina. "It'll never happen!" he barked, delighted to draw a chorus of boos.

Terrell sprinted toward Sammy, forcing him to backpedal. Terrell cocked the ball back in his left hand, winding up for a vicious toss. He let the ball slip at the last second, fooling Sammy, who had spun to avoid a throw that never came. Terrell caught the hovering ball and bounced a vicious throw in one motion. The rubber projectile landed just behind his quarry. Ever fleeting, Sammy gathered himself and leapt skyward. The little waterbug would've gotten away if the force of the ball's momentum hadn't caused it to bounce off the floor and hit him in the backside. Terrell smiled, bowing to boos and moans from the audience, pleased that his unbeaten streak had survived.

Terrell began to feel weak soon after the game ended. He realized that exercising with such vigor after having just come off a drunk wasn't the smartest thing he'd ever done. He told Officer Smith that he needed to leave early.

He felt glad not to have a long wait for the bus. His forehead sweated from more than just the hot weather as he exited minutes later. He struggled through the four block walk from the bus stop to his apartment complex, wondering if he looked as bad as he felt.

Upon arriving, Terrell felt surprised to see a certain sporty little car parked in front of his apartment building. A certain girlfriend who should have been out of town stood beside it.

VI

"I thought you weren't comin' back until Friday?" Terrell said.

"And I thought you might be in some kind of trouble since I haven't heard from you since this past Friday morning," Monet said. A mixture of anger and relief colored her pretty face.

Terrell hugged her before taking her hand and leading her to the building's entrance. "Let's talk inside."

Monet sat on Terrell's couch a few moments later. He poured the last of his orange juice into a glass for her.

"Thank you." She tilted the glass to her full lips. They were as gorgeous to him as ever, as was the rest of her. As beautiful as she was, her good looks were almost secondary to her kindness and pleasant personality. How could he have cheated on such a great catch so easily?

The hard look in her brown eyes informed Terrell that she was about to let him have it. "Why haven't you called me and why haven't you returned any of my calls or messages? I was worried sick about you!"

"I'm sorry, baby." Terrell tried his best to sound innocent. "You know salesmen are always callin', gittin' on my got damn nerves! I guess I turned the ringer off 'n' forgot to turn it back on."

"I don't think that's a good excuse, Terrell," Monet hissed. "If you weren't getting my calls, you should've taken the initiative to call me. Weren't you thinking of me?"

"Of course, I was thinking of you, baby." Terrell took her hands in his. "The truth is I've been sick all weekend. I think I ate a bad hamburger or somethin'."

Monet stopped complaining and gave him a once over. "You do look a little worse for wear," she admitted. "Have you been to a doctor?"

"Naw," he snickered as if she had just asked the silliest question in the world. "I've just been takin' Pepto Bismol and drinkin' a lot of fluids."

Monet laughed. "Oh, I forgot. Black men don't like going to the doctor unless they're on their deathbed."

"Damn right," Terrell said, winking at her. "And I'm as black as they come."

"Boy, you're light skinned!"

"I'm light brown."

"Whatever you are, it certainly isn't 'as black as they come'. And don't get cute." Monet shoved him, only half playing. "I'm still mad at you. I drove more than five hours, through crazy traffic just to come check on your silly behind. You need to get yourself a cell phone! This is 2001.You know- the 21st century."

"A cell phone ain't in the budget, baby."

"Not even a pre-paid?"

"Nope. Can't see it."

"Why don't you let me get you one?"

"Nahhhh. That's a big step down the road to being a kept man. Can't have that. I just couldn't live with myself."

"I hate you." Monet frowned, shoving him again.

"I love you, though." Terrell leaned across the couch and puckered his lips.

Monet laughed and planted a kiss on him. "You get on my damn nerves."

"Yet you can't resist me."

She shoved him a third time. "That just proves that I must be crazy."

Terrell soon found himself listening to Monet talk about her time in Virginia Beach. It was just run of the mill family stuff, but he was happy to hear it. He could have listened to her talking about the family barbecue for days, as it served to keep him from thinking about his actions during the same time frame. Once she tired of talking about southern Virginia's version of the Huxtables, Monet began to kiss Terrell. Those kisses started out tender before blooming into something far more passionate, far more urgent.

"Are you feeling well enough to give me a homecoming present?" she purred.

Terrell smiled. "I think I'm well enough to sit back and let you do your business."

Monet did her business very well.

VII

The braying of Terrell's alarm clock murdered his slumber at 3:30 a.m. He dragged himself from bed, prepared to start his trip down to the fish trucks by catching the number 5 bus. A bleary eyed Monet would have none of it. She insisted on driving him down to the docks at the Inner Harbor. He relented, but would not hear of her staying up so that she could drive him back.

Terrell hated everything about his second job- the hazy darkness before dawn of the pier, the rude chill birthed by the Patapsco River, the redness of his hands from handling the icy fish.

What he hated most was heading home clad in the smell of halibut from head to toe. Still- he made $50 cash, twice a week for his troubles, for two hours work. He had to work about 20 hours to bring in the same amount of money from Americorps, $3000 educational stipend be damned.

Terrell wouldn't see that funding until he logged 900 hours and even then, he would have to use it toward educational expenses. That made the money he brought in from pitching fish vital income. As he played catch with that morning's disgusting bounty, Terrell felt relieved that Monet believed his excuses for not making contact with her. This was one occasion when lying was far better than telling the truth.

After finishing his smelly work, Terrell walked the five or six blocks from the pier to the nearest number 5 bus stop. It happened to stand on Baltimore's infamous Block. The red light district stood vacant and lifeless during early morning hours. Still, the lurid advertisements of its storefronts and strip clubs promised a wealth of seedy vices that would reach their peak during the coming night. Terrell had no doubt that the fishy stench that clung to him disgusted his fellow early morning bus riders. He thought he must smell like the contents of a dumpster outside of Phillip's seafood restaurant.

"You home, baby?" Monet called from the bedroom after he entered his apartment. The husky tones of sleep filled her voice.

Terrell kissed her on the forehead before removing his reeking clothes and taking them to the laundry room across the hall. He climbed back into bed after taking a much needed shower.

Monet awakened him with a kiss at 11:00. "I dried your clothes for you, sleepyhead," she said. "Are you working at the P.A.L. center this afternoon?"

Terrell rubbed his eyes. "You know it."

She sighed. "I wish you didn't have to work so hard."

He shrugged, getting to his feet. "It's part of life."

"So is loving a knucklehead like you," she said, mussing his short afro. "What time are you going in?"

"One o'clock."

"Cool. That gives me time to pick up some groceries before I drop you off. Your kitchen is almost bare and what is in there hardly qualifies as real food. I don't know what you'd do without me."

*Oh, nothing much*, Terrell thought. *Just got caught up in a triple murder*. "I'd be a sad, sorry individual."

"Aw, that's so sweet," Monet pinched his cheek. "You really know how to pour it on- you know that?"

She dropped him off at the P.A.L. Center as promised. She also came to pick him up at the end of his shift. Well to do family, as nice as could be- she was quite the girl to have in his corner. Before the events of two nights past, Terrell might have thought he deserved someone like her.

Once more his conscience assailed him with the assertion that if he had only been true to her, the horrible events of that night would not have happened.

VIII

Terrell felt as surprised as Monet did when Brock and Shawntae came by. As always, they greeted her as if she were the queen of the manor. When she asked about his bandaged hand, Shawntae told her that he had cut himself making a sandwich.

"You know he's lyin'," Brock joked. "Chubbs here almost gnawed off his own arm in a feedin' frenzy. Tha's what really happened."

Monet chuckled. "That's not nice," she said, poking Shawntae's stomach as if he were the Pillsbury Doughboy. "And he's not chubby. Just a little plump."

"That's right," Shawntae agreed. " 'N' I still get more love from the ladies than you, milk dud."

"Wow, Tae." Brock pretended to be amazed. "Milk dud? I've neva heard that one before. And it makes so much since cuz I'm dark skinned. You're s-ooo clever."

"Whateva, you little ink blot."

As Monet busied herself with preparing a spaghetti dinner, Brock and Shawntae motioned Terrell toward his bedroom.

Brock whispered in Terrell's ear once they were inside. "We gotta meet 'n' talk bout 'n' alibi- just in case those chicks eva turn up."

"You think that's possible?" Terrell matched his cousin's low volume.

Brock shrugged. "I don't know what's possible no more."

"Where do y'all want to meet?"

"At the Apex on Broadway," Shawntae responded.

"What the hell for?" Terrell snapped, realizing that Shawntae had asked to meet at a seedy porno theatre. He clapped a hand over his own mouth, regretting raising his voice.

"Keep it down," Brock said, placing a forefinger over his own lips. "Why you think, man? Anybody who's there ain't gon' be payin' attention to what the fuck we're talkin' about."

"Aight, man," Terrell said, nodding his agreement. "We'll do that shit tomorrow night. I'll ask my girl for the car."

"Cool," Shawntae said. "Le's meet up around 9."

They heard a knock on the bedroom door. Terrell tried not to look like he had just knocked over a 7-11 as he opened it. "Wassup, Mo?"

"I just wanted you to come taste the meat sauce." Monet's smile did nothing to mask the skepticism in her eyes. "Terrell if you're on the down low, I'd like to know before we get married."

They all laughed.

"Your girl got jokes," Brock said.

"I'm just saying," Monet continued, "three guys in a bedroom, all quiet and stuff. What's really going on?"

"Just a little man talk, baby," Terrell said.

"Man talk? I hope that's all it was. I hope you guys weren't tweezing each other's mustaches or something."

The three conspirators laughed as they left the bedroom. Monet laughed too, though suspicion remained in her eyes. She returned to the kitchenette, shaking her head at their strange behavior.

The pleasant aroma of the meat sauce wafted through the apartment as Brock and Shawntae took their leave. Shawntae paused at the door to joke about staying for the meal.

"You wish," Monet said, laughing and rolling her eyes. She gave Terrell a once over after his visitors departed.

"What?" he asked.

"You're not hiding anything from me. Are you?"

Terrell smiled and held his hands up as if he had been ordered by police. "You got me, Mo. You're not gonna let it go, so I might as well confess. The fellas and I are planning to rob a bank."

Monet frowned. "Very funny. Keep it up and I won't share any of this good food with you."

IX

The Apex Theatre stood alone as a first run triple XXX theatre in Baltimore. If not for the white marquee that screamed ALL NEW ADULT

MOVIES in big black letters, the brick building might have gone unnoticed amid the bar and restaurant dominated landscape of its' trendy Fells Point neighborhood.

The seats in the lone auditorium were old and rickety, as if the place hadn't been renovated in 50 years. The smell of cleaning fluids permeated the auditorium. Two nerdy-looking middle aged guys huddled at opposite ends of the rearmost row were the only patrons to share the seedy locale with Brock, Shawntae, and Terrell.

The three young men settled into the third row from the front, paying little attention to the sights and sounds of world class smut that emanated from the big screen in front of them. "I can't believe you're eating popcorn in here," Terrell said. Shawntae sat between him and Brock.

"Why not?" Brock responded, smacking his lips. "I'm hungry. Besides it smells like they clean this place wit' Lysol every hour or some shit."

"Whateva," Shawntae said. "You kin keep eatin' that sperm corn, if you want to."

Brock whispered, "We're not here to talk about my eatin' habits. Besides, you know you really down wit' the hairy palms squad. You problee jerk off as much as you eat." He cackled. 'N' you know tha's a lot o jerkin' off."

"Yeah-and you'd problee like to go back there and watch." Shawntae grinned, pointing his thumb over his shoulder toward the two serious viewers. "Wouldn't you? You don't have to hide it, Brock. You know you wanna go back there and watch those white boys squirt race."

"This ain't no time to play," Terrell growled. "Shit is all fucked up and y'all wanna tell your little high school jokes?"

Brock sighed. "I knew you was gon' start trippin. Look, cuz - You're right for thinkin' that shit is all fucked up. But it ain't like we're gon' to jail or no shit like that."

"What makes you so sure about that?"

"For one thing," Brock spoke between smacks of popcorn, "Them girls ain't neva gon' be found. We did that shit too smooth."

Shawntae put his hand on Terrell's shoulder. "He's right. The bodies will never be found. Why would anyone ever just happen to comb Lake Montebello?"

Terrell nodded. "You got a point. But by now those girls have been declared as missing persons."

"We know that," Brock said. "We also know they'll problee make the news or at least the paper, any day now. Tha's why we need to git our story straight about what we were doin' that night, right now."

"Yeah?" Terrell shrugged. "So what's the story?"

Shawntae grinned. "Iss a beautiful thang, T. Them bitches ran the streets so much that we don't need to make up nothin' special. Them chicks coulda been wit' anybody."

"I know tha's right," Brock agreed. "Them hoes done problee been wit' a hundred niggas apiece."

Terrell's face flushed with anger. "So whatchu sayin'-Brock? You sayin' iss cool to do them in cuz they were freaks?"

Brock scowled as he answered. "You know I don't think that shit was cool." Though he kept his voice low, his gesticulating arms confessed his frustration. "Whatchu think? You the only one feelin' guilty? You can't be feelin' half as guilty as I do. I'm the one who did the shit."

"You sure are," Terrell said, glaring at his cousin. "You are the one who killed those girls."

"What the fuck, man?" Brock jumped up, heading toward Terrell. His seat shrieked in protest as Tae wrestled him back into it.

"You think you better than me, cuz?" Brock said, struggling to break free. "You got somethin' you wanna git off ya chest?"

"Shut the hell up before you git us kicked outta here." Shawntae spoke with a calm that belied his words and forceful restraint of the smaller man. He then turned and shot Terrell a look that warned him not to say anything else. "Don't keep doin' that shit to him, man. You think he needs you to remind him what the fuck he did?"

"No." Terrell looked away. "No, I don't." He leaned across Shawntae after a few moments, making eye contact with Brock. "I'm sorry for carryin' it like that, cuz."

Brock shrugged. "It's cool. I jus' want us to stick togetha. Tha's all."

"We are gon' stick togetha," Shawntae said. "We're gon' stick togetha jus' like we always have. Right now we need to git our alibi straight like we came here to do."

"Yeah," Brock said, nodding. "Jus' in case our names ever do come up wit' the cops."

"Y'all are right," Terrell agreed.

They decided that if the cops ever came around, they would tell them that they had all gone to a late movie at White Marsh that night. They would say that the original plan had been to cruise by some clubs after they let out-to see if they could hook up with any girls. They'd say that the plan had never materialized because it had been raining so hard when they got out of the movie theatre. Instead, they drove back to Terrell's apartment where they sat up drinking and playing video games. They'd say that the weather had been so terrible that Brock had to pull to the side of the road a few times during the trip back.

It was a plausible story and one the cops couldn't disprove without hard evidence. As Tae said, those girls were the kind who might have been with anyone that night. Also, the cops wouldn't be able to deny the severity of the weather, since it had been the worst storm of the year so far. The only thing that bothered Terrell was that his neighbor Mr. Johnson might have seen Tia when Brock answered the door. Brock assured him that there was no chance of that, saying that he had only cracked the door to talk to the guy.

"Besides," Brock joked, "That old hid woulda broke his fuckin' neck trying to get a better look if he caught sight of a little tasty like her. Shorty looked fat as shit that night."

They left the theatre after settling on their story. As they departed the darkened auditorium, one of the serious customers approached them along with the theatre employee who'd sold them their tickets and served Brock his popcorn. Both of their faces were red with a mixture of annoyance and fear.

Brock snickered. "Don't bother," he said. "We're leavin'."

Despite the plausibility of their story and the improbability of the girls' remains ever being found, worry wracked Terrell as he drove home. He sat alone in Monet's car for a long time after reaching his building, not wanting to face her until he could at least pretend to be calm.

# Chapter Three

I

Two days passed without incident after the meeting at the Apex. Terrell went to work when he was supposed to and hung out with Monet in his free time. He didn't speak with Brock and Shawntae. This was an unusual occurrence since Monet had come into his life. He huddled with her on his couch, watching the 10 o'clock news on Fox 45 when a female reporter spoke the words that brought his relative piece of mind to a crashing halt.

"Police are seeking information about three missing teenaged girls from the Waverly-Govans neighborhood. Two sisters, 18 year old Tiffany and 17 year old Tia Jenkins have been missing since last Friday evening. Their eighteen year old friend Heloise Hopkins is also missing. Heloise is believed to have been on her way to meet the sisters when she was last seen."

The television screen split as the reporter spoke. School photographs of all three victims occupied the right half. The sweet, almost innocent images of the pictures portrayed nothing of how wild they'd all really been.

"If you have any information that might assist the authorities in finding these young women, please contact the missing persons hotline on your screen. Callers may choose to remain anonymous."

Terrell shook his head. "Tha's a damn shame."

"Yeah," Monet agreed. "Hopefully some crazy person hasn't chopped them up or something like that."

II

A furious wind howled, blowing strong enough to shake the colossal trees that consumed the landscape as far as Terrell could see. Its' unrelenting fury threatened to knock him to the ground. Terrell broke into a run, wanting nothing more than to escape the endless forest that stretched before him.

As he ran, Terrell's feet began to feel as if he were running in thick mud. He looked down and saw that what felt like mud was a swamp of coagulated blood. The trail of blood stretched as far as the forest itself.

Mr. Howling Wind started to blow objects loose from the multitude of trees. Terrell realized in horror that the objects were the decapitated heads of Tia, Tiffany, and Heloise. Thousands of them fell, matching every step that he trudged forward.

Discolored and malformed from underwater decay, the horrid stench of the heads caused Terrell's eyes and nose to run. Pus, mucus, maggots, and worms splattered from each one as they struck the ground with sickening thuds. Terrell covered his face as he ran, not wanting to see the horror.

He stepped on one of the decayed heads, lost his balance and fell to the ground. Blood and other disgusting fluids he couldn't identify splattered his body as he struggled to his feet. He heard the drone of flies start as a distant hum, growing louder with each frightened breath he drew.

Terrell soon realized that it was not flies he heard. It was the voices of the heads, both falling and fallen. They spoke as a thousand fold chorus.

"Why didn't you help us?" They droned. "Why didn't you help us? Why didn't you help us? Why didn't you help us? Why didn't you help us? Why didn't you help us?"

The voices grew louder and louder, until Terrell's ear drums ruptured. Blood leaked from them as he again lost his balance. A lack of equilibrium caused him to fall twice more before he managed to right himself. To his dismay, he could still hear their voices inside of his head.

"Why didn't you help us? Why didn't you help us? Why didn't you help us? Why didn't you help us? Why didn't you help us? Why didn't you help us?" They droned, sounding as if every fly that had ever flitted on a carcass during the millions of years of Earth's existence had gained the power of speech.

Terrell stopped trying to run and covered his oozing ears. "There was nothing I could do!" He screamed. "There was nothing I could do! There was nothing I could do! There was nothing I could do!"

"…Baby." Terrell heard a distant voice. "Wake up."

"There was nothing I could do."

"Wake up." The voice grew closer. He realized that it sounded familiar.

"Wake up." Terrell felt himself being shaken.

He opened his eyes, struggling to register that Monet was the person shaking him. It took him a moment to process the fact that he was in his own bed, with his own outstanding catch of a girlfriend. Monet maneuvered herself behind him, wrapping her arms around his lean torso. "Are you with me now, baby?" she asked, her dulcet voice soothing him.

"Y-yes," Terrell stammered.

"You were having a nightmare. It must have been a horrible one, too. I've never seen you like that." She lowered him onto his back, placing a hand over his sweat drenched chest. "Your heart is beating so fast! You've had a terrible scare." She kissed him on his wet forehead. "Don't move. I'll get you some water."

Monet attended Terrell with a tenderness he felt he didn't deserve. He felt relieved that she didn't ask any questions, although he knew full well that she was burning to know what had gotten into him. A new and terrible fear emerged as they lay beside each other.

"Did I say anything while I was having that nightmare, Mo?"

Terrell's stomach lurched when she nodded. "You kept screaming that there was nothing you could do. You screamed it over and over."

Monet stared at him, waiting to see if he would explain himself. When he didn't; she sighed and kissed him on the cheek. "I'm going back to sleep," she said. "You should, too."

"I don't know if I can."

She stroked his cheek, speaking in a soothing tone. "Baby, I'm right here. It's okay. If you have another bad dream, I'll be right here to comfort you."

"I know you will, Mo," he said, kissing her on the cheek. "You're a good woman. You know that? Right now, I feel like I don't even deserve you."

She giggled. "Of course you deserve me, silly. You're a great guy. You're smart, you're nice, and you always do the right thing." She pinched Terrell's cheek, having no idea that her words intensified the guilt that stabbed at his soul. "Now get some sleep, Terrell Hawkins."

"Yes, Ma'am."

Terrell pretended to sleep just long enough for Monet to doze off. Then he lay alone with his guilt, staring at the ceiling.

III

Terrell spoke with Brock and Shawntae the day after the girls were declared missing. They all agreed that there was nothing to worry about; that it wasn't unusual for people to go missing in Baltimore. If they were ever pressed about whether or not they had seen the girls that night, they'd just give the alibi they'd rehearsed. They doubted that things would even get that far. Once the cops found out what kind of girls the victims had been, they were sure to assume that they all had turned ho or something.

Though he still struggled with guilt about his role in what had happened, Terrell felt confident that they wouldn't be caught. As Brock had assured him, murder can't be proved without a body, physical evidence, or reliable witnesses. The cops who investigated this case would have none of those resources.

Terrell had never been more grateful of having Monet in his life. He relished every moment with her, for time with her was time with the demons of fear and guilt kept at bay. When he wasn't with Monet, he threw himself into his work at the PAL Center and at the fish carts. When not doing any of those things, he sometimes found himself hanging out at the Parkside Shopping Center Giant grocery store. There he performed the kind deed of helping old ladies load groceries into their cars.

Keeping busy kept Terrell's demons at bay. He fell to the bottle to still his tortured mind when he couldn't find any other adequate distraction.

After they discussed the discovery of the bodies, Terrell didn't answer his phone whenever Brock or Shawntae's numbers flashed on his Caller ID. Talking to them would serve to provoke images of what had happened on that terrible night. He imagined that they were living the same lives they had been living before the murders. That meant working, drinking, and trying to catch some easy pussy whenever possible.

Maybe Tae was working his way back into his baby mother's good graces. He and Darlene had been on and off again since tenth grade, the main reason being the big man's failure to keep his dick in his pants. Whatever Brock and Tae were up to, Terrell was sure they were doing it with a lot more comfort than he felt.

Brock didn't seem too torn up about what had happened. Maybe the little guy was holding it in, but the fact that his cousin could be so composed after having murdered three people disturbed Terrell to no end. He wondered if he had ever really known Brock as well as he thought he had. He would never have imagined Brock doing what he'd done before it happened. Terrell hoped never to find out what else Brock was capable of doing in an effort to save his own ass.

IV

On Saturday June 25$^{th}$, Terrell took his younger brother Terrence to the movies for an early birthday present. The little guy's actual birthday fell on the following Monday, but Terrell had to work that day.

Terrell loved hanging out with his little brother. The little guy looked up to him so much that he even imitated his mannerisms. Their father had died in a construction accident when Terrence was 4 and their mother had never remarried. Those circumstances resulted in Terrell becoming the closest thing to a father figure that Terrence had ever known.

Terrell was only twelve years old at the time of his father's passing. He had to wear a man's shoes after it happened. He drew on everything that his father had instilled in him to become a strong role model for his younger brother.

Seated behind the wheel of Monet's car; Terrell felt ashamed about the admiration that Terrence regarded him with. He had always taken great pride in that admiration before. But then before, he'd felt that he deserved it.

"When I get older I wanna be a pimp jus' like you," the little guy said, smacking on some popcorn that was left over from the movie.

"I ain't no pimp, boy," Terrell said, frowning. "Why you talkin' crazy?"

"I don't mean pimp like with prostitutes, big brother. I mean pimp like that could get my girlfriends to do nice stuff for me."

"You mean like lettin' you drive their tight whip?"

"Yup."

Terrell held his fist out for Terrence to pound it.

"Damn. I guess I am a pimp then."

"Yup." Terrence grinned. "But I'ma be a better pimp than you when I get older."

"How you gonna do that?"

"I'ma get a girl to let me drive a Hummer."

Their brotherly banter continued until they reached their mother's split level rancher. It was a beautiful three-bedroom home in a picturesque neighborhood near the Baltimore/Rosedale line. All these years later, Terrell still couldn't look at it without considering that money from his father's death benefit had paid for it.

Terrell stopped in for a bit to talk with his mother. As always, he marveled that she looked so young and beautiful for someone who worked so hard and had lost the love of her life. The uninformed might have thought she was his older sister. Mrs. Hawkins implored her son to stay a little longer, complaining that he didn't come by enough.

"I know," Terrell said, smiling and kissing her on the cheek. "One day we'll go out, jus' me 'n' you."

Mrs. Hawkins frowned. "Sure we will. You always say that."

"Sorry, Ma." Terrell shrugged. "I'm a busy man."

"Too busy for your own mother?"

After managing to extricate himself, Terrell drove to pick Monet up from one of her friend's apartments. He pelted her with kisses as soon as she settled into the passenger seat. "I want you bad," he said.

The smile that bloomed on Monet's face promised mischief. "Well, then- drive fast."

V

While Terrell and Monet had at each other, Brock sat alone in his room at his grandmother's house. Having just polished off a 40 ounce and a chicken box, he was set to go prowling for a new sexual conquest when an emergency news break caught his attention.

"This is Charles Dolan of WBFF-TV 45 News," the reporter said. "We interrupt your regularly scheduled broadcast to bring you breaking news here from Lake Montebello."

The dapper reporter stood at the edge of the fencing that separated Lake Montebello's shore from its running/bike trail. A great number ofpolice vehicles dotted the landscape. Brock didn't need to hear anything else Mr. Dolan had to say to get the gist of what had happened. He listened anyway.

"In the grey light of dawn, a local fitness enthusiast leaned over part of this fencing while stretching at the conclusion of his daily run. Upon doing so, he noticed a dismembered and partially decomposed head lying at the foot of the reeds that grow along the shore. He promptly called the police, whom immediately mobilized a team to drag the lake once they confirmed the sighting. The dragging operation revealed the dismembered remains of three young women. Although the remains still need to be identified, it is believed that they are those of Tia and Tiffany Jenkins and Heloise Hopkins, the three young women whom mysteriously disappeared from the Waverly-Govans neighborhood a few weeks ago. Police expect to be able to confirm the identities of the victims within 24 hours. Mayor O'Leary and Police Commissioner Harris are expected to hold a special press conference tomorrow to address this grisly matter."

"Fuck!" Brock screamed. "How the fuck kin this happen?"

"Watch your mouth in there, boy!" his grandmother yelled from the hall.

"Shit," he muttered, thinking for the ten thousandth time that the walls of the house were too damn thin. "Sorry, Granma!"

Brock turned off the TV and listened for the creaking floorboards to tell him that she had gone down the hall, into her bedroom. Once he heard the faint sounds of gospel float from her room, he knew that she wasn't coming out anymore that night. Heart and mind racing, he went for a drive. Hard as he tried, he couldn't make sense of how one of those girl's heads had floated ashore. They had disposed of the chopped up bodies too perfectly. They had even weighed them down.

Brock recalled Shawntae once claiming that only an act of God would result in their victims ever being discovered. *Maybe that's what happened,* he thought. Well, Brock didn't care about God's acts or what God wanted. He wasn't going to prison for the rest of his life or facing the needle for nobody, not even the great spook in the sky. He never could stand church, no way.

He blamed Tia for everything that had happened. *That fucking bitch,* he thought. *If only she hadn't gone off like that, none of this would have happened! That crazy bitch made me do what I did. As far as what happened with the other two, that was just a matter of survival.*

After realizing that he had been driving like a wild man, Brock pulled the Cutlass to the nearest curve. He turned on his hazards and sat with the car idling until he was able to collect himself.

He thought of rousing Terrell and Shawntae, but he knew that Monet and Darlene would have a lot of questions if he dragged their men away out of the blue on a Saturday night. Darlene was sure to be the most suspicious, since she'd just started to get tight with Tae again. He had to play it smarter than that.

Brock decided to wait until the morning to get the others on the phone. With sex having become the least of his concerns, he decided not to go trolling for pussy after all. Another 40 ounce would do him just fine instead.

VI

Brock woke up early on a Sunday for the first time in ages. He felt alert and focus, despite all the drinking he'd done on Saturday night.

He sat up on his bed and grabbed the remote from his nightstand. He turned the television on, expecting to get an update about the girls' bodies. Sure enough, the well appointed Mr. Dolan interrupted a televised church service to do the honors. Not a hair stood out of place on his majestic head.

"We interrupt your local broadcast to inform you that the remains of the three girls found in Lake Montebello have now been identified. As previously reported on this station, a jogger stumbled upon a decayed head along its shore early yesterday morning. Police subsequently dragged the lake and have now used forensics and family identification to confirm that two of the victims are 18 year-old Tia Jenkins and 17 year-old Tiffany Jenkins. The sisters are formerly of Cator Street and Argonne Drive in the Waverly-Govans area. They are survived by their mother, Glenda Carter, and their older brother, Wendell Smith. The third victim, Heloise Hopkins, age 18 was a close friend of the two sisters. Mrs. Hopkins lived on East 43rd street, also in the Waverly-Govans area. She is survived by her grandmother, Hattie Gomes, and her mother, Alicia Gomes. The three victims had all been missing since Friday night, June 10th. The Baltimore Police Department is promising to use all available resources to solve this case as its shockwaves ripple through the Greater Baltimore Community. There have been as yet unsubstantiated rumors that the FBI may become involved. We have just confirmed that Mayor O'Leary and Police Commissioner Harris will hold a special press conference within the hour to address this horrific issue. Stay tuned to this station for continued coverage of this horrible development."

Brock did just that, waiting until the station's cameras panned to Police Headquarters downtown to begin dialing his potential co-defendants. A makeshift podium stood in front of huge entry doors that bore the Baltimore Police Department insignia. The podium bore a seal that read The City of Baltimore.

Tae answered the phone in a groggy voice. "Wassup, man?"

"Bad shit, man," Brock said. "Turn on the news. I'ma click over 'n' call Terrell."

"Aight, man," Tae said, sighing. He hadn't been watching the news but he knew that Brock calling so early was not a good sign. Brock clicked back over when he heard Terrell's phone ring, starting a three way call.

"You there, nigga?" he asked Tae.

"Yeah, man."

Monet answered Terrell's phone on the third ring. "Hello."

"How you doin', sweetheart?"

"Wassup, Brock?"

"Nothing much, baby girl. Is your man up? I'm sorry to call so early, but iss kinda important."

"Hold on."

A few moments later, Terrell grumbled, "What do you want, cuz?"

"Git away from your girl right now, man. Turn the news on. I got Tae on this line, too."

Terrell excused himself from Monet and walked into the living room. Silence permeated the three phone lines as each caller watched the Mayor and Police Commissioner's press conference unfold. The city big wigs looked authoritative, determined, and very displeased. Promises were made to spare no resources in bringing the girls' murderers to justice. Chills traveled up all three of the conspirator's spines.

Brock ended the stunned silence. "Y'all remember the alibi we made up?"

"Yeah," Terrell and Shawntae answered in unison.

"Good, cuz we might need it."

They ended the call then. All three of them felt terrified about what might come next.

VII

Monet awakened Terrell just before dawn on Monday morning. The droning chorus of the girls' dismembered heads had violated his sleep again, leaving him alarmed and shivering. Monet comforted him and brought him water, making certain that he regained his composure before she began to probe him.

"Terrell, baby," she said, pecking him on the cheek, "You keep having these nightmares."

He nodded. "I know."

"I think you're traumatized about something. You obviously don't want to tell me, so maybe you should see somebody."

Terrell's red eyes widened. "You mean like a shrink?"

"I mean like a therapist."

Terrell frowned. "I'm not crazy, Mo."

She hugged him. "Baby, I know you're not crazy. You don't have to be crazy to need somebody to talk to. I just don't want you to keep having these nightmares. You don't deserve to suffer like this."

"How kin you be so sure?"

"What?"

"How kin you be so sure I don't deserve to suffer like this? How kin you be so sure I don't deserve worse?"

Monet moved away from him and stood in front of the bed. "You're acting really strange, baby. This is not you. Would you please go see somebody?"

"Sure," Terrell said, smirking and getting to his feet. "I'll go see somebody. Jus' like Miss Monet wants. Miss Monet with the doctor for a daddy and the lawyer for a momma. I'll bet Miss Monet would have no problem payin' for it, either. Miss Monet loves to provide charity for poor little Terrell. Her very own Baltimore boy."

Tears welled in Monet's eyes. "What the hell is wrong with you, Terrell?" she screeched. "Whatever it is, you have no right to be so mean to me. I've done nothing but love you and be good to you!"

The pain in her voice and truth in her words caused Terrell to feel ashamed. He had attacked her for caring about him. What kind of asshole does that? He felt disgusted with himself.

He threw his arms around her, hugging her like a scared toddler clinging to its' mother. "I'm so sorry, baby. I'm so sorry, Mo. You're right. I need to see somebody. I'm not quite right."

"So you will see someone?" A hopeful smile dawned as she wiped her tears and submitted to his embrace.

"Yeah," he agreed, willing to say anything to placate her.

"Alright, then. I'll arrange it." She squeezed his cheek. "I'm not trying to give you charity, Terrell. I just want to help you."

He attacked her with a flurry of small kisses, causing her to giggle. "I know you do, beautiful. Forget I said all that stuff. Okay?"

"Alright," she said, sucking her teeth. "I'll forgive you, this time."

Terrell felt pleased that he hadn't pushed Monet away as his conscience screamed for him to do. He believed that he no longer deserved her, but he also believed that he was sure to crumble without her.

VIII

Terrell was watching Judge Greg Mathis when a newsbreak interrupted the program. To his dread, reporters spoke with Tia and Tiffany's grief stricken mother and brother. Morbid curiosity kept him glued to the screen.

"I knew it was them," their mother sobbed. "From the time those bodies were discovered I knew it was my girls. The police just proved what I already felt. Somebody killed my babies and chopped them up like they were…like they were chicken parts or something. They didn't deserve this. Nobody deserves this."

The woman's son placed her sobbing face upon his shoulder. Violent trembling racked her body as her words fragmented into incoherent sobs and gasps. The female reporter stuck a microphone into the son's gaunt, tired face, giving no consideration to his efforts to comfort his mother.

"Do you have anything to say about the tragedy that has befallen your family, Mr. Smith?"

"Yes." The young man's raspy, baritone voice trembled, complementing the anguished expression on his face. "I just want to say - I just want to say that if anybody out there knows anything, please come forth. Whoever did this to my sisters and their friend don't deserve to walk free. This could have been anybody's sister, anybody's daughter. If you know anything, please come forth."

More of the same followed when reporters interviewed Heloise's grief stricken family members. Just thinking about the fact that she'd been murdered just after he had sex with her made Terrell's stomach lurch.

He became aware that his ragged breathing stood a hair away from hyperventilation. Beads of sweat dotted his forehead as he sought relief in the liquor cabinet. He drank straight from the bottle, the burning sensation of the liquor staving off a panic attack.

Terrell felt relieved that Monet was in the shower. Her sharp mind might have started to put things together if she had seen how he reacted to the newscast. He'd much prefer for her to think he was coming unraveled for some unknown reason than to suspect even a shadow of the truth. He had allowed Monet to schedule an appointment with a therapist for him later in the week, but he knew that wouldn't result in him feeling any better. He couldn't even tell the shrink what the real problem was. What was he going to say, "Doc, I can't sleep because I'm an accessory to a triple murder?"

No, he couldn't do that. He had a few days to think of a good charade to try to put one over on the talking head. If he couldn't think of something good enough, he wouldn't go at all. He knew that shrinks were good at mind fucking people and he was almost bursting with guilt. He couldn't risk letting something slip.

Terrell resigned himself to keeping his tormented thoughts deep down inside. Having his conscience eat at him was a terrible thing, but he knew that circumstances could be much worse. He felt blindsided and mortified when they become that way.

# Chapter Four

I

It took every iota of Terrell's fortitude to keep from pissing his pants on the afternoon of Wednesday, June 29th. The homicide detectives that came to his job were the source of his bladder issues.

Terrell knew their business as soon as they walked through the gymnasium doors. They were dressed in sharp but practical suits and they each possessed a confident gait that bordered on arrogance. One of the pair was tall and thin. His shaved head and dark skin gave him a slight resemblance to a young Michael Jordan. The tall man's middle-aged partner stretched average in height and portly in width. He had sharp blue eyes and thinning blond hair.

Terrell continued to help some kids during Summer Reading hour, pretending that he didn't notice the detectives' presence at the far end of the basketball court. The one who inspired thoughts of Michael Jordan motioned to Officer Smith. Terrell saw recognition light in Smitty's eyes as he left the kids he was working with and approached the two men.

Terrell returned his attention to the little boys and girls gathered at his table, modeling how to use expressive voices while reading. He saw the detectives leave the gymnasium when he dared to glance over a minute or so later. Relief washed over him. He allowed himself to entertain the notion that they had not come for him after all.

That flicker of hope was extinguished when Officer Smith called him into his office a few minutes later.

"Close the door," Officer Smith said. The grave look on his face told Terrell that what he was not about to share good news. He suppressed an urge to take off running before Officer Smith spoke another word.

Officer Smith cleared his throat before speaking. "There are some detectives outside who want to question you, Terrell. They're homicide detectives."

Terrell feigned shock. "What the hell would homicide detectives want with me?"

A slight quaver invaded Officer's Smith's voice. "Did you know those three girls who were found in the Lake?"

"Hell no!" Terrell snapped, locking eyes with his interrogator.

Officer Smith sized him up. "Well, those detectives seem to have reason to suspect you did," he said. "Luckily for you, I graduated from the academy with one of those guys. I convinced them to wait for you outside, instead of calling you out in front of the kids, making you look bad and contributing to parents feeling like it's no longer safe to bring their kids to this P.A.L. Center. I want you to go with them and take the rest of the day off when you're done. Don't worry. I'll make sure you get paid for the whole day."

"What will I tell the kids?"

Officer Smith shrugged. "Tell them you had to take your brother somewhere for his birthday. They'll believe anything you say. They all look up to you." His eyes narrowed when he made that last statement.

"Okay." Terrell started to leave the office before thinking better of it and turning to face the man he knew as Smitty. "You believe me-don't you?" he asked, pleading with his eyes.

Officer Smith nodded. "Yes. I think- no, I know you're one of the better people I've known. So if you say you didn't know those girls, I believe you. I just hope whoever did those terrible things gets caught soon. I tell you, I'm sick that it happened right across the way from here. And this is supposed to be a safe place for kids. This is the sort of thing that could result in the city relocating the center or even closing it down."

For the first time, Terrell pondered how far reaching the ramifications of the murders were. Sure, he'd seen the makeshift shrine of mylar balloons and teddy bears hung on the lake's fencing. He also knew that a candle light vigil had been held for the slain girls at the lake on Sunday night. But he had yet to ponder the damaging affects of the bodies being discovered so close by on the school and P.A.L. Center.

Now that Officer Smith had spoken of it, Terrell realized that there less kids than usual in the center that day. With school out for the summer and working parents needing a daytime shelter for their young children, attendance should have been higher. The fact that it confirmed Officer Smith's concern that a significant number of people no longer felt safe about sending their children to the Montebello P.A.L. Center. Terrell had played a huge part in that development.

“Try not to worry too much, Smitty,” Terrell said, placing a reassuring hand on one of the officer’s broad shoulders. “Things will be better once they catch whoever did it.”

“I hope that’s soon, Terrell.” The lawman rose from his seat. “When things like this happen, I almost wish I had chosen to become a detective. That way I could help catch the scum who did it.”

“Come on, Smitty,” Terrell said, smiling. “If you were a detective, you couldn’t be the patron saint of Montebello Elementary School.”

Officer Smith laughed and slapped Terrell on the back. “You’re right,” he said. “You’re a good man, Terrell. I don’t know how they got your name, but I know those guys are just fishing. Still, you’d better not keep them waiting any longer.”

II

Terrell stood on the sidewalk, about 20 yards away from the school’s towering entrance. He found himself face to face with what he thought of as a salt and pepper Laurel and Hardy, but he knew this was no comedy. He knew right away that of the two, Black Laurel/Young Jordan was the only one young enough to have been Officer Smith’s academy classmate.

“Terrell Hawkins I presume,” Laurel spoke first, extending a hand. Terrell decided that it would be best to appear cooperative, giving Laurel a cautious shake. The thin man’s pale-skinned partner did not offer his chubby mitt, scowling at Terrell instead. Right away Terrell knew that he was about to be treated to the old good cop-bad cop routine.

"Yes." Terrell pretended to be bewildered. "What can I do for you, Detectives…?"

"I'm Detective Douglass and this is my partner, Detective Dunbar," the thin man said, motioning to the tub of lard. "We hate to disturb you at work, but…."

"Why are you being so damn polite to the guy?" Dunbar interrupted, his voice as gruff as his partner's was melodic. "We're here to question him, not make friends."

"Yes, we are here to question him," Douglass responded, seeming to measure his words. "But he isn't a suspect."

Dunbar smirked. "Not yet."

"What the hell does that mean?" Terrell scowled, continuing his pretense of ignorance. "What would I be suspected of?"

Dunbar pulled his suit jacket open, giving Terrell a good look at his badge. "That there says we're homicide detectives, Ace. So we ain't here investigating a B and E. That's for sure."

Terrell widened his eyes, pretending to be shocked. "I don't know anything about any homicides!"

"Maybe. Maybe not," Dunbar said, smiling like he had the goods on Terrell already. "Lemme ask you this. Did you know Tia and Tiffany Jenkins? What about Heloise Hopkins? Did you know any of those girls?"

"That doesn't sound like…," Terrell began, acting out a slow realization. "Wait a minute- you think I know those three girls that were found in the lake? I didn't know those girls!"

“Are you sure about that?” Detective Douglass spoke in the tone of a curious friend.

Terrell nodded with vigor, causing his chin to meet his clavicle. “Yeah, I’m sure. I never met those girls. I don’t know where y’all got that idea from.”

Dunbar stroked his own double-chin. “Maybe we got it from your cousin, Damon Brock.”

Terrell realized that he would have to be very careful during this exchange. Detective Douglass and Detective Dunbar seemed well practiced at the double team and he had watched enough Law and Order to know that detectives wouldn’t hesitate to lie in hopes of tripping up a suspect.

“Naw,” Terrell said. “I don’t believe that.”

“What’s not to believe?” Detective Dunbar said. He shrugged his beefy shoulders. “He said you, he, and your buddy Shawntae Kennard had ‘fucked around’ with those girls before. Now you’re saying you’ve never met them. So that leaves two questions. Which of you is lying – and why?”

“He couldn’t have said that, cuz I don’t ‘fuck around’ with nobody but my girlfriend,” Terrell barked. “I’m not just some dumb nigga, by the way. I don’t believe he said that shit just because y'all say so.”

Detective Douglass smirked. “Dumb ‘nigga’ or not, can you tell us where you were on the night of June 10th?”

Terrell gave them the story just as he and the others rehearsed it.

“So that's your story,” Detective Douglass asked, a bemused expression on his face.

“That's the truth.”

"I got another question for you," Detective Dunbar said, fixing Terrell with a stare. "Why don't I believe you?"

"No, I have a question for you guys," Terrell fired back. "Am I under arrest?"

A look of defeat dawned in Detective Douglass's eyes. "No – you're not under arrest," he said.

"Then I have nothing else to say to you… detectives." Terrell summoned the harshest glare he could muster before turning to walk away.

"We're not through with you, yet," Dunbar said. "We'll talk to you again."

"Whatever," Terrell snickered, not bothering to turn around. "Good luck with your investigation." His brain kicked into overdrive as he crossed the street to his normal bus stop. Feeling a nice summer breeze, he opted to bypass public transit and walk down the hilly part of Erdman Avenue. He passed Mother's Garden, the lush example of botany that had been commissioned by former Mayor William Donald Schaefer to honor his late mother, long ago. Terrell paid the beautiful sight no mind. Nor did he feel an even momentary appreciation of the Clifton Park golf course whose immaculate expanse unfurled less than one hundred yards to his right. His one track mind traveled only in the direction of his encounter with the detectives. As his heart rate increased from the fast pace of his walking, he decided that the detectives had lied about Brock in hopes of getting him to spill something. Divide and conquer was one of the oldest tricks in the book. They would need better bait to hook him.

Douglass and Dunbar were far too well versed in the art of lying and tripping up suspects to say that Brock had told them Terrell had something to do with the killings. Instead, they told Terrell that Brock had admitted to them spending time with the victims and sat back to see if he would be dumb enough to spill anything.

The "fucking around" part even sounded like how Brock talked. But Terrell knew that it would have been stupid of his cousin to point the detectives toward him and Tae. Apart from them all being like brothers, Brock couldn't risk pissing his cohorts off because they were the only ones who could confirm that he'd killed those girls. Brock wouldn't want to get into a situation where it was him or them. Besides, the three of them had a plausible and well-rehearsed alibi for that night, one that the cops couldn't disprove.

Terrell felt certain that Brock had stuck to the story they'd come up with. After questioning Brock, the cops must have decided that he, Terrell, and Shawntae had a united front. That's why they'd tried to make it seem as if Brock had set them on Terrell's trail, in hopes that Terrell would take the bait and incriminate his cousin. Terrell knew that the detectives would try the same act on Tae, if they hadn't done so already. He also knew that they would only get more of the same response from the big fella.

The cops would need better bait to hook any of them. If the bastards had anything real, one or all of them would have been in custody already.

Terrell was so lost in thought that the almost two mile walk home seemed like much less. He concluded that Brock was the one the police suspected as he entered his apartment, wiped sweat from his brow, and poured a glass of water. What he couldn't figure out was why they suspected Brock.

After all, Brock and Tae hadn't been around Tia and Tiffany before that night. They had been trying to hook up for a while, but it hadn't worked out. It's not like they were some of the other dudes who had been seen around with the girls. So of all people, why did the cops suspect Brock? Terrell knew his cousin had done the shit- but that's only because he was there when it happened.

Terrell wracked his brain until he remembered that Brock had called the girls on his cellular phone that night. *That's why the cops are looking at him,* Terrell concluded. *Probably the first thing the police did was pull recent phone records. They could get that kind of information without a problem and when they did, Brock's number turned up. If that's the case, things aren't that bad yet. If the police are basing their questioning on phone records, they've probably questioned at least ten other dudes from that night alone. Those girls got around.*

Terrell's belief that the cops were fishing solidified. They were on a big expedition, trying to make a bunch of suspects nervous and see who would panic. The pressure to pin the crimes on someone, anyone- had to be tremendous.

The case had made national news and just as Brock had cautioned, the mayor had taken a tough stance on crime. His star was sure to shine a lot brighter if he could brag that such horrible murders had been solved under his leadership.

Well, Detective Douglass and Detective Dunbar would have to do a lot better than they had so far. Terrell didn't think that they'd ever get anything more than the record of Brock's cell phone to go on.

III

Terrell heard alarming intensity in Brock's voice when he called that evening. "Did anybody come to see you?" he asked.

"Yeah."

"Shit, man," Brock said. "They came to see me early this mornin'-before I even left for work. They came to see Tae, too. Meet me at Herring Run, by the bridge."

"Alright."

Terrell felt relieved that Monet had an evening summer school. Her determination finish her undergrad degree as soon as possible saved him an explanation of where he was going. He exited the number 33 bus across the street from the park's northern entrance, then hot footed it toward the agreed upon meeting place.

Terrell knew that Brock was spooked because he hadn't offered to pick Terrell up, perhaps thinking that the cops were tracking their movements. It was possible, but Terrell thought it was far too early in the game for that. Terrell walked past the park's basketball court, ignoring the frenetic game of shirts and skins in progress.

Brock and Shawntae stood under a bridge in the center of the park's bike/jogging trail, one on each side of its' graffiti-marked underpass. Terrell didn't like them being there before him. He wondered if they had been talking about him. Maybe they had been considering whether they thought he'd hold up to police pressure.

Terrell dismissed that notion as soon as it was born. Why shouldn't Brock and Tae be there before him? After all, he had placed himself on the outside of their circle by avoiding them since that terrible night.

When Terrell got close, Brock whispered, "Nobody followed you- did they?"

That question confirmed Terrell's belief that his cousin was paranoid. "How could somebody follow me on the bus, cuz?"

"Don't take nothin' lightly. They're on us, now."

"They're not on us. They're jus' fishin'."

"I wish I could be that confident," Brock said, his eyes wide. "But fuck it. Le's talk about how all our conversations wit' those pigs went."

After they each recounted their encounters, Terrell found his theory confirmed. The cops found out that Brock had spoken with the girls through phone records. Brock had stayed cool, giving them their rehearsed alibi about being at White Marsh on the night they were last seen, running his smart ass mouth at the same time. He told the cops that he had called Tia and Tiffany, but they had faked on him that night. Unable to shake Brock, the detectives had decided to see how Tae and Terrell would react if they said that Brock had admitted to them hooking up with the girls before.

Shawntae breathed a sigh of relief. "It ain't really nothin' to worry about, then," he said. "They jus' fishin'. Like Terrell said."

Brock shook his head in disagreement. "Naw, man. I think iss more to it than that."

"Like what?" Terrell asked.

"I saw Tia and Tiffany's brother at the Cedonia Inn late Monday night. He was in my class for a minute at Lake." Brock referred to Lake Clifton High School, which stood less than a mile from Lake Montebello.

"Oh, that nigga went to Lake? I thought I had seen yo before when he was on the tube," Tae said. He frowned. "So what? You saw him at the Cedonia Inn. You can't blame that dude for drinkin' his pain away."

"He was drinkin' it away, alright," Brock said, nodding. "He was fuuucked up. I told him how sorry I was about everything that happened. Even offered to cop him a 40. That's when he started actin' real crazy."

"Crazy how?" Terrell asked.

"The muthafucka started talkin' 'bout how he didn't believe in God no more since his sistas died. He said he won't rest until the muthafuckas who killed his sistas is rottin' in a cell or in the ground. Said he thought it might've been one of the niggas he saw all the time around B-More. He even told me that he thought I mighta been involved for a minute. At first, I thought he was jus' talkin' off his ass cuz he was all drunk and fucked up in the hid. But then them homicide cops popped up at my crib the next mornin'? That ain't no coincidence, y'all."

"It *is* a coincidence, Brock," Terrell said. He wasn't sure if he believed so, but he needed to convince his cousin. There was no telling what Brock might do otherwise. Witnessing the way he had dispatched those girls made Terrell think him capable of anything.

Brock looked away from the others, pacing back and forth like an expecting father in a hospital waiting room. The next words he spoke informed Terrell that he had flown over the cuckoo's nest. “I might as well tell y’all. I’m thinking about takin’ Wendell out. That’d shut his fuckin’ mouth.”

“Are you stupid or somethin’ Brock?” Terrell hissed. “You got to be stupid.”

“Don’t be calling me stupid, Terrell,” Brock snarled, pointing at his cousin. “Don’t call me stupid, nigga.”

Terrell’s facial expression grew just as furious as his cousin’s. “You are stupid, nigga!” he yelled. “You wanna wipe out the whole family, now? Is that it? You like killin’ people now?”

“I jus’ said I’m thinkin’ about it, man. I gotta do somethin’.”

“You don’t have to do shit!” Terrell screamed. “Your crazy ass has done enough, already!”

A middle aged jogger who was approaching them stopped for just a second, startled by Terrell’s belligerence.

“What the fuck you lookin’ at, Old Man?” Terrell roared. “What the *fuck* are you lookin’ at?”

The jogger turned beet red, almost falling as he turned in flight. Terrell tore off after him.

"I'll teach you to mind your fuckin' business!" he yelled as he ran. He felt like he was outside of himself, watching someone else's crazy deeds. Brock and Tae grabbed him just before he could reach his quarry.

"Calm down," Tae groaned as they held him fast. "Calm down, Terrell. You can't do shit like that."

Terrell began the gradual return to his own body. As the rage that had possessed him left, his breathing slowed to a normal pace.

"We betta git the fuck outta here," Brock said, keeping his eyes fixed on his cousin. "Somebody problee called the cops."

Terrell stared holes into the back of Brock's head as Brock drove back to Terrell's apartment. "You'd better not do anything to those girls' brother," he growled. "He doesn't know anything. That was jus' drunkness 'n' pain talking."

"Brock ain't gonna do shit," Tae said. "He ain't gonna do shit because he knows that would only make shit worse. Ain't that right, Brock?"

Brock nodded, speaking in a flat tone. "Yeah, man. That was jus' talk. I'm jus' skeered, tha's all."

"Erybody's skeered," Tae said. "But iss like Terrell said- the cops are jus' fishin. If they had anythang, we'd all be in cuffs right now. So there's no need for nobody to do nothin' rash. All we gotta do is stick to our alibi 'n' erythang'll be fine."

Shawntae's wary eyes panned the car, inspecting each of his cohorts. Terrell realized that Tae felt as if both he and Brock might be going crazy. Maybe the big guy was right to think that.

"Alright, fellas?" Tae pleaded.

"Alright," Brock and Terrell agreed, their respective tones grudging.

Terrell didn't trust Brock not to do anything rash. He didn't trust Brock at all anymore. He began to think of his cousin as a personal threat. He wouldn't have been surprised to learn that Brock felt the same way about him.

IV

Terrell's roommate called him a few minutes after he entered his apartment. Talking with Malik provided a welcome diversion from Terrell's tormenting thoughts. Malik claimed to be having a grand time in New York, chasing girls and making good money conducting surveys for his uncle's public health agency.

"I'm glad my uncle was able to pull some strings to get me the gig," he said. "It's a lot better than that courier shit I did last summer."

"I'll bet it is," Terrell said.

"Hell yeah it is. Anyway, son- you should come check me for a couple of days. I'll show you what the rotten apple is all about. You down?"

"I don't know, man. I got some shit I gotta deal with down here."

"We all got shit to deal with, wherever we are, Baltimore. That shit ain't life or death- is it?"

"Naw," Terrell lied.

"I-ight, then. Come check me when you straighten that shit out. You haven't seen NYC until you've seen it with Malik Patterson."

Terrell chuckled. "Is that right?"

"That's right, man. You could come out this weekend. Stay 'til at least Monday. That's the Fourth of July. Show you how we celebrate that shit up here. You'll have a ball, son. I'm tellin' you."

Terrell considered Malik's offer after their conversation ended. He thought that leaving for a few days might be just what he needed. But doing so might make those detectives more suspicious of him if they came to question him again. Terrell still felt convinced that Douglass and Dunbar had been going through the motions of casting a wide net the first time they'd come around. Terrell figured that he, Brock, and Shawntae were just another trio of fish in the deep blue sea of the detectives' investigation. They were far from prime suspects, but if the detectives got wind of Terrell leaving town they might assume that he was running from something and ratchet up their focus on him. Terrell wasn't about to do anything to attract any more attention. He hoped that Brock and Shawntae would keep their profiles as low as he intended to keep his.

V

A week passed without Terrell hearing from or about the detectives. He breathed a little easier, figuring that he might not hear from them again. He felt fortunate that Officer Smith didn't seem suspicious of him. Being suspected at work would have been too much for him to handle.

A small part of him couldn't help feeling concerned that Smitty might be playing possum. After all, a cop was a cop and they all stuck together, as far as Terrell knew. Still, if Officer Smith's detective buddies weren't after Terrell, why would Officer Smith be? After all, he'd said that he believed

Terrell didn't have anything to do with those girls and Terrell hadn't even registered a cross look from him since the detectives came to the P.A.L. Center.

Terrell mastered his anxiety enough to embrace the routine of working and spending time with Monet. She didn't need to work because of her parents' money, but she was enrolled in three summer school classes at Morrison. When they were both free they did the usual things that young lovers do. That included hanging out, lots of conversation, and a whole lot of sex. They celebrated the Fourth of July Monday in bed together, resting and enjoying each other bodies. They laughed at the sounds of their neighbors setting off fireworks in the street. When nightfall approached, Monet drove through horrible traffic down to the Inner Harbor. They watched the city's annual fireworks show on the waterfront. Back at Terrell's apartment, they had at each other once more as the crackling sounds of bottle rockets and the like continued outside.

VI

While Terrell passed time with Monet, Shawntae made serious progress toward reconciling with Darlene, the mother of his two year old.

He had lost all appetite for womanizing after what transpired on June 10th. He'd promised himself that he would try to live a better life since that horrible night. Reducing his drinking and carousing were serious steps in that direction.

Like Terrell, Shawntae believed that Detective Douglass and Dunbar had only been reaching when they tried to put the squeeze on him and his cohorts. He felt that the cops would find themselves with just another cold case on their hands if he, Terrell, and Brock continued to play it cool. The rub was his lack of confidence that Brock would so.

Unlike Terrell, Shawntae still kept frequent contact with Brock. Although Shawntae had lost all enthusiasm for hanging out with the little murderer, he made it his responsibility to keep Brock close. What he saw in his friend worried him. Brock's words seemed to be slurred every time they talked on the phone. Twice, he sounded like he was good and drunk before the evening sky began to darken.

"I hope you ain't turnin' into a alcoholic," Shawntae grumbled during one of those occasions.

"Heyyyy, Don't worry about me," Brock slurred. "I'm straight as kin be. Ha! That rhymed. Don't worry about me, big boy! I'm jus' livin' a little."

Brock could play the merry drunk all he wanted, but Shawntae was not fooled. He knew that a fearful and desperate soul lay beneath that exterior, a desperate soul whom had already killed three times. He worried that Brock might still try to do something to Wendell Smith, although he had promised otherwise. He drummed discouragement of such foul action into his friend's ear every time they talked. He never referenced the situation in explicit terms, having decided to act on the worst case scenario assumption that the cops were on their asses and had tapped their phones. He doubted that they had, but there was no sense in not being as cautious as possible.

"You're not going to mess wit' that lil bird – are you?" He asked during one such phone conversation, making an uninspired attempt at coded language. "Messing wit' that bird kin only bring more trouble."

"For the last time, Tae," Brock sighed, "I'm not gon' do nothin' to the lil bird. I ain't even worried about that fuckin' bird." Judging by the even, steady quality of his voice, Shawntae seemed to have reached him during a rare bout of sobriety.

Brock seemed sincere every time that he issued a coded denial about wanting to harm Wendell. He seemed even more sincere when they saw each other in person and spoke in plain terms. Still, Shawntae couldn't shake the feeling that something very bad was about to happen.

VII

Brock believed that Terrell and Tae were right in telling him that killing Wendell Smith would be the wrong thing to do. Doing so would make him look more suspicious and he didn't want to be responsible for the deaths of all three of some poor woman's children. He hadn't wanted to be responsible for the death of anyone, but that bridge had already been crossed and burned down.

If only that stupid bitch Tia hadn't attacked him. He was only fucking around and she ended up dying. As for the others- What was he supposed to do? Leave those bitches in one piece so he could be carted off to jail? Why should he go to jail because some raunchy whore got hurt while trying to attack him?

Such thoughts plagued Brock whenever he was alone, time after time, drink after drink. He was drinking far more than he ever had and he hadn't been within the same galaxy as a teetotaler to begin with. He guessed that it showed, because Shawntae was now watching over him as if he was his fucking mother or something. The big man made it obvious that he was worried sick that Brock might do something to Wendell. Brock told Tae time and again that he wouldn't touch the boy, but he just couldn't get the big man to believe him. What Shawntae didn't know was that Brock had set his malicious sights on someone else, someone Brock meant to eliminate without either of his cohorts knowing.

VIII

One of the scores of decent, hard-working men who lived in Baltimore City had left his second job well after dark on Thursday, July 7th. On Tuesdays, Thursdays, and Saturday evenings the solid citizen put in 4 hours teaching technician training classes. His day job paid fine, but he was trying to save up enough money to buy a house.

The tired man completed a 30 minute drive through the city by parking his van in front of his apartment building. He locked its doors before walking up the front steps. The parking lot was empty of people, though it teemed with parked vehicles. He didn't feel surprised that the residents of the apartment complex were all inside enjoying their air conditioners because today had been one of the hottest days of the young summer. Even at this hour, the temperature threatened ninety degrees outside, a heat that was augmented by stifling humidity.

The man stifled a yawn as his foot hit the second step. At that moment, a masked assailant leapt from the bushes. A single shot fired from a snub nosed .38 revolver blew a hole in the side of the poor sap's face. A towel that had been placed over the gun's barrel muffled its report. A small flame flared at the towel's end as the ejaculated bullet tore through it.

As his victim tumbled to the concrete, the assassin removed the towel with his gloved left hand. He took a second towel from his waistband and wrapped the gun's barrel once more.

The second muffled shot entered the victim's brain through his forehead, extinguishing his already fading life force. The assailant dropped the second towel and rifled through the slain man's pockets, taking his wallet but not bothering to check it for money. He stomped the towels to make sure that they no longer burned before stuffing them back into his waistband. Damon Brock was long gone before his fourth victim was discovered.

# Chapter Five

I

Monet and Terrell headed back to his apartment after catching a movie at Beltway Movies 6. The second-run theatre stood in the center of a strip mall on Belair Road, a few blocks past the county line. Terrell anticipated another night of good sex after their cheap date ended.

His worries about going to prison for his involvement in those girl's deaths had decreased with the passing of time. He allowed himself a sliver of hope that things wouldn't turn out all bad. Sure he'd have to live with his horrible guilt, but in time he might atone for what he'd done in other ways. He also thought that his strong relationship with Monet just might be enough to keep him sane.

Terrell's hope abandoned him after Monet turned into the parking lot of his apartment complex. She rounded into his court, revealing a swelling crowd engulfed in murmured excitement. It was the sort of gathering that people most often did in the aftermath of something terrible. The young couple saw police cars parked in front of Terrell's building, lights flashing. A line of yellow caution tape extended from the front door to the middle of the asphalt parking lot. A dead body lay at the very edge of the interior of that tape, sprawled out at the bottom of the steps that led to the entry door. Harsh crimson stained the ground around the covered form.

"I want you to git out of here," Terrell said.

"What?" Monet asked.

"I want you to git out of here," he repeated, his tone stern. "Someone's been killed 'n' I don't want you around this stuff. Now I'm gonna git out of the car and you git out of here."

"But what about you?"

"I live here, baby. I'll find out what's goin' on, then I'll call you back to come git me. Maybe I could chill witchu tonight."

"But-"

"Do what I say, Mo! You're not meant to see shit like this."

"And you are?"

"You'd be surprised at what I've seen." He leaned across his seat and kissed her forehead. "Now, go on and git outta here."

Terrell exited the car, not needing to look back to know that Monet was watching him walk away. Relief washed over him as he heard the sounds of her driving off a few moments later. He crossed the parking lot and fell in among the crowd as policemen struggled to keep observers from getting too close.

A large man cried out in despair, asking what the world was coming to.

"Yeah, that shit is fucked up," a young man seconded the sentiment. "Right in front of our building."

"That nice man didn't deserve that," an elderly woman pitched in her two cents. "It's getting so decent folk aren't safe, anymore."

"Who is that?" Terrell asked.

The elderly woman's spectacled eyes remained fixed on the scene in front of her as she answered. "That's Mr. Johnson- that nice gentleman who worked for BGE. Someone shot him on his way in from work. Why would somebody do that to such a nice man?"

II

Everyone else might have scratched their heads about who would want to kill Mr. Johnson, but Terrell knew who the guilty party was. He concluded that Brock had thought about the fact that Mr. Johnson saw him at Terrell's apartment on that terrible night and decided that maybe the poor guy had gotten a glimpse of Tia on the couch. So Brock had eliminated what his paranoid mind saw as a liability.

Terrell felt complete understanding of his cousin at that moment and that understanding terrified him. Brock had become more paranoid and more dangerous with each passing day. Brock had also gotten used to killing. He'd kill anyone if he thought it might save him from going to jail.

The desperate fool hadn't stopped to consider the likelihood that killing someone who lived in Terrell's apartment building would lead to the three of them becoming stronger suspects. After all, Baltimore wasn't the biggest city in the world, nor did it have the largest police force. Cops in Baltimore knew each other, as was the case with Detective Douglass and Officer Smith. Terrell hung around the crime scene long enough to see that Dunbar and Douglass had not been called to it.

Still, he knew that sooner or later they would hear about it. Their suspicions of he and his cohorts would grow even stronger then. Even worse, they might think that Terrell had committed or at least helped arrange this particular murder. After all, the victim had been his upstairs neighbor.

Terrell's alibi of being with Monet at the time wouldn't deter Laurel and Hardy from chasing that angle. After all, the pressure was on for all branches of the law to solve the "Lake Montebello murders". The case was just another black eye for Baltimore on the national scene, as if being among the perennial leaders in violent crime, drug addiction, sexually transmitted diseases, and failing public education were not enough.

After the body was carted away and all possible physical evidence was gathered, the cops allowed residents to enter Terrell's apartment building. Terrell walked to the Cedonia Inn and purchased a half-pint of Wild Turkey before doing so. He drank like a desert traveler stumbling upon an oasis, straight from the bottle. The burning in his throat and chest managed to stave off sensory overload.

His thoughts having slowed to a manageable speed, Terrell decided that he was ready to confront Brock. The crazy little bastard had to be brought under control before he did anything else.

III

The three accomplices stood under the bridge in Herring Run Park. Terrell checked his wristwatch and found that midnight approached. He was sweaty and short of breath, having speed-walked the mile and a half from his apartment to the meeting place. The park's night lights shone for fifteen second intervals every minute or so, bathing him, Brock, Shawntae and their surroundings in a golden hue before fading back into darkness. A soundtrack of chirping crickets and croaking frogs serenaded the three young men.

Terrell took several deep breaths, steeling himself for the impending confrontation.

"Alright, we're here," Shawntae said. "You want to tell me why you made me have to leave my baby mova so late? Shit, I've been gittin' in good wit' her lately. Now she thinks I'm off tryna fuck some bitch."

"Ask him," Terrell answered, pointing at Brock. "He knows why."

Brock raised his right eyebrow. "What the hell are you talkin' about?"

"Don't play stupid, Brock," Terrell growled. "Nobody here is stupid."

"I know that," Brock said, a smirk on his face. "Except maybe Tae. He ain't neva been that bright."

Terrell lunged at Brock, only to be caught and restrained by Shawntae.

"You wanna tell jokes, you fuckin' psycho?" Terrell screamed. "You wanna act like nothin' is wrong? You're full of shit, Brock! I know what you've done!"

The park lights shone at their brightest as Brock scowled. "The fuck you talkin' 'bout, yo? You goin' crazy, man."

"Oh, tha's beautiful. That is really beautiful." Terrell clapped his hands. "I'm the one who's goin' crazy? I'm the one who's goin' crazy? Let me go, Tae. I ain't gon' do shit to this dude. It ain't worth my time."

"You swear you ain't gon' do nothin'?"

Terrell held his hands up in surrender. "Yeah, man," he said. "I ain't gon' do nothin'."

Shawntae released him, keeping alert for any sudden moves.

"I ain't gon' do shit, man. All I'm gon' do is talk."

"Well, talk then," the big man said. "Let us know why you got us out here."

"I could do that. But it would be better if Brock told you. You wanna tell 'im Brock?"

"You're not makin' sense, T," Shawntae grumbled.

"I'm not makin' sense to you, Tae. That's because you don't know what happened." Terrell glared at Brock. "Since the cat seems to have my cousin's tongue, I'll fill you in."

"Alright." Shawntae raised an eyebrow in curiosity. "What is it?"

"Remember my upstairs neighbor, Mr. Johnson? The dude who worked for BGE? Somebody killed him tonight."

"Wha-at?" Brock said. "Man, tha's some crazy shit."

"Cut the bullshit, cuz! I know you did it. You did a nice job, too. Straight assassinated his ass right in front of the building. Nobody heard any gunshots, either. No witnesses. I don't know how you pulled that off. I guess you nigga rigged some kinda silencer, cuz I know you couldn't a bought a real one. Then again, you're in the streets more than I am, so maybe you could git your hands on the real deal. Whatever the case, the first person who saw him was some dude leavin' out his apartment to go work the graveyard shift. My guess is you had your car parked in a back alley nearby. You even knew exactly when he'd get home. You must have been plannin' it for at least a couple days. I guess you were worried that he might have caught a glimpse of Tia on the couch when he came to the door that night. You know, right before you killed her." Terrell slapped Brock on the shoulder in a mock admiration.

"Congratulations, cousin. You're a true blue killa now! You're gittin' really good at killin' people- especially those who haven't done a thing to you."

"You're losin' it," Brock said. "I don't know how you got that crazy idea in your hid. Yo, the stress must be gittin' to you, cuz."

"Oh, you're right about that," Terrell snickered, pointing his left index finger. "You're got damn right the fuckin' stress is gittin' to me. And all of that stress is your fuckin' fault. But that doesn't mean I don't know what the hell I'm talkin' about. You're actin' like you're so surprised that I'm sayin' this, as if you weren't jus' talkin' about killin' those girls' brother cuz you thought he knew somethin'. If you felt that way- why wouldn't you git around to thinkin' you had to kill Mr. Johnson- who definitely saw you that night?"

Brock shrugged. "Man, that was jus' skered talk when I said that shit about Wendell," he said. "I'm sorry somebody killed your neighbor, but it damn sure wasn't me."

"Really?" Terrell moved closer, jabbing his pointed finger against Brock's chest. "Well if you didn't do it- who did? Who else would want to kill him?"

"How the fuck should I know?" Brock's voice rose as he pushed Terrell's hand away. "You betta git the fuck out my face, man! You ain't no cop. I don't have to be interrogated by you."

"You're right. You don't have to be interrogated by me. But I'll problee have to be questioned by the cops again, especially since you murdered someone who lived upstairs from me, you stupid muthafucka!"

"This is a buncha bullshit," Brock said, smirking and turning to Shawntae. "You don't believe any of this bullshit? Do you, big fella? I mean-this dude must be losin' his fuckin' mind!"

"I don't know, man," Shawntae said, anguish filling his voice. He held both palms out in front of his body. "I don't know what to believe."

Brock's face twisted into a sneer. "I can't believe you jus' said that! You gonna listen to his ass?"

Shawntae scowled. "Yeah? Well, I can't believe you killed those girls in the first place. I would've neva believed that could happen."

The emerging park lights illuminated Brock's face again. His eyes stretched wide, in a mixture of anger and disbelief. "So iss like that? Well fuck you then, you fat muthafucka! Tha's how y'all wanna play it? The two of y'all against me?"

"If we were against you, we would've gone to the cops already," Shawntae said.

"Maybe we should've," Terrell muttered.

"What the fuck did you jus' say?" Brock yelled. "What the fuck did you say?"

"You heard me, you fuckin' psycho!"

"Yo, y'all chill out," Shawntae said. "We gotta figga this shit out."

"There ain't shit to figga out." Brock pointed at Terrell. "This bitch ass nigga is actin' like he wanna snitch now. 'N' for what? Cuz he got a guilty conscience?" He stared daggers at his cousin. "You ain't do shit to stop what happened that night, so don't try to act like you betta than me now. Let the real man keep handlin' shit, you fuckin' pussy!"

The park lights fell away, leaving harsh darkness again. Terrell grabbed an unsuspecting Shawntae by the shoulders, slinging the larger man to the ground. He took advantage of the clear path to deck Brock with a vicious left cross. He climbed astride his cousin then, getting in several hard punches before Tae recovered and dragged him off.

"Stop, Yo!" Shawntae shoved Terrell. His considerable might toppled the slighter man. Terrell righted himself and attempted to renew his assault, but Shawntae blocked his path with a nimbleness that would make Jonathan Ogden proud.

"I done had enough of you, cuz," Brock said, getting to his feet and wiping his bloody lip with the back of his hand. "You really want to fuck wit' me?" He reached into his waistband, revealing the same handgun he'd used on Mr. Johnson. "You really want to fuck wit' me?"

Shawntae's eyes threatened to pop from their sockets. He twisted his massive body into a mighty push of Terrell, sending Terrell into a brief backward flight. Before skidding backwards across the asphalt, Terrell looked like a man whom had jumped back first from a first floor window.

"Stay the fuck ova there!" Shawntae bellowed. "Stay the fuck ova there! I'ma try to smooth this shit out. This shit ain't gotta go this way."

The big man sized Brock up, trying to gauge how to approach the situation. He said, "Why you pointin' a gun, Brock? You don't wanna shoot nobody-do you? I mean, I know you 'n' Rell go at it sometimes, but you don't wanna shoot 'im. You can't want to shoot 'im."

"I don't wanna do nothin, Tae," Brock said, keeping the gun poised at chest level. "I didn't come here to shoot nobody. But I ain't lettin' him beat my ass, eitha."

"Ain't nobody gon' beatcha ass. He gon' stay ova there."

"Muthafucka I…," Terrell growled. His palms were scraped from sliding across the asphalt.

"Shut the fuck up, Terrell!" Shawntae shouted him down. He rushed his attention back to Brock. "He gon' stay back. I'ma come ova there 'n' see how hurt you are."

"I'm aight, Tae."

"Naw, you ain't," Shawntae said, shaking his head. "You bleedin' pretty good. I' ma come ova there 'n' see how bad you hurt, tha's all I'm gon' do. My hands are out. You see I ain't got nothin'- right?" Holding his palms out, he inched toward Brock. It seemed that things might work out alright when the smaller man lowered the gun.

"I look that bad?" Brock asked. He spat out a wad of the blood that trickled from his mouth. A large strawberry sprouted high up on his right cheek.

"Yeah, you look pretty fucked up. Even uglier than usual."

"I should a beatcha ass worse," Terrell grumbled. "Pull a fuckin' gun on me. After all this shit?"

"Shut the fuck up, Terrell!" Shawntae bellowed again, the park lights bathing his furious face. "Don't say nothin' else! You ain't helpin' the situation! You actin' like a fuckin' crazy person." He returned his gaze to Brock. "Damn, Brock." His voice grew calm again. "You need stitches. We should take you to the hospital."

"Iss that bad?"

"Iss that bad, man. Lemme hold that gun for you so you kin git cleaned up."

Brock spoke in a tone that bordered on clinical. "I ain't givin' you this gun, Tae."

"Brock you can't go in the hospital wit' a fuckin' gun," Shawntae argued.

Eyes wide, Brock growled, "I'll leave it in the car or somethin', but I ain't givin' you this gun."

"I'm so sick of this shit!" Shawntae howled. Darkness surrounded them once more. "What you need a gun for, Brock? Iss only us!"

"Iss only y'all? Tae- do you see what that muthafucka jus' did to me?

"Yeah, I did that shit," Terrell said, heaping kindling upon the fire. "I wasn't finished witchu eitha." He darted toward Brock, his situational insanity not allowing him to consider that his actions might bring about more tragedy.

"Stay the fuck away from me, Terrell!" Brock raised the gun, eyes wild with fear. "Stay the fuck away from me!

"What the fuck, man?" Shawntae said. "Point that shit down!"

"I ain't pointing sh-" was all that Brock managed before Shawntae grabbed the gun with one and Brock's wrist with the other.

"Gimme the gun, Brock," the big man demanded, attempting to wrench the weapon away.

"Get the fuck off it, Tae!" Brock yelled, resisting with all his strength. "Let it go."

"No!" Shawntae bellowed, intensifying his effort to take the weapon. "You let it go!"

A booming report resounded through the night as the two combatants tumbled to the ground. The park lights re-emerged at that moment, illuminating the carnage before Terrell. As Tae lay on top of Brock, Terrell saw his cousin's eyes grow wide. Noticing how Tae's body slumped, he realized that the larger man had been shot.

"Aw fuck, man. Aw fuck," Brock gasped, as Tae's blood spilled onto him. "I didn't mean to shoot you. I didn't mean to shoot you, Tae." A tortured wail escaped from Brock, interrupting the night song of the crickets and frogs. "Terrell!" he cried. "You gotta help me! You gotta help me! I didn't mean to do that shit!"

His intentions were of no consequence to his fallen friend.

IV

Shawntae lay motionless save for the violent heaving of his chest as he struggled for breath. "You gotta help me," Brock groaned, struggling to roll his wounded friend off of him.

Terrell stood frozen, hands clapped to his temples in anguish. He realized that it was his fault Tae had been shot. If he hadn't attacked Brock, Brock might not have pulled his piece. Things might have still been different if he had not approached Brock a second time. What the fuck had gotten into him?

Terrell saw the murderous metal lying a few feet from Brock's right hand, within easy reach for him, but even easier reach for Brock. He knew that grabbing it was the only way to control the horrible situation that confronted him. He also knew that he would never make it to the weapon before Brock did. What then?

Having shot Tae by accident, was Brock now capable of doing in his own flesh and blood? Terrell didn't doubt that his cousin's desire for self-preservation was that strong.

He thought about running away. Brock remained pinned underneath Tae and that would give him plenty of chance to get a head start. He could flee down the bike trail and through the woods. He'd figure out his next stop once he was safe. Terrell came very close to doing just that as the park light's cycled through, plunging the nightmarish scene before him back into abysmal darkness.

He stayed because running would guarantee Tae's death. He hoped that something might be done to save the big man. As Terrell remained frozen in place with his mind on overdrive, Brock managed to roll Tae free.

"Help me," he pleaded, his breathing labored. "He's still alive."

Brock rose to his feet and gathered the revolver, tucking it into a rear pocket of his jean shorts. Shirt painted with fresh blood, he used the back of his left hand to wipe sweat from his brow. He followed by wiping his bloody mouth and gums. He scored a hat trick of gruesomeness by spitting a second glob of blood onto the ground.

"Oh, shit, T," he moaned. "He got popped in the stomach."

Blood painted Shawntae's fingers as he pressed them against his abdominal area. The crimson fluid coated the asphalt around the big man. His breath came in an aria of pathetic wheezes.

"Oh, no," Terrell whimpered. "Oh, no."

"Stay wit' me, Tae," Brock pleaded, leaning over his fallen friend. "Stay wit' me."

Shawntae moaned something unintelligible as his eyes rolled to the back of his head.

"Shit, he's goin' into shock!" Brock wailed, slapping Shawntae's face. "Stay wit' me, big man! Stay wit' me."

Shawntae's pupils returned from the void into which they'd disappeared. The brown pupils strained at the sockets that held them, bulging like those of a hungry owl that upon spying a field mouse. His irises were filled with far too much red. He lost a pained struggle to speak, producing only a wounded moan. Twin streams of blood trickled from the corners of his mouth, falling upon the dark asphalt.

Brock stood up. "Shit, man. He's done for."

"What?"

"You heard me." Tears streamed down Brock's face, rushing to meet the blood that marred the collar of his tee shirt.

"There's nothing we kin do for him?"

Brock shook his head. "No, cuz. Look at 'im. All we kin do is let him die slow."

"We could take him to a hospital."

Brock smirked. "Take him to a hospital? The fuckin' ride would problee kill him."

"You could call 911."

"On my cell phone? You know they'd trace that shit. Besides, he's all fucked up! By the time they made it out here, he'd problee still be gone 'n' we'd both end up in jail to top it off. The cops would connect all this shit for sure. Then we're talking the rest of our lives in prison or the fuckin' needle. Do you want that?"

"No, I don't want that," Terrell said, tears salting his eyes. "But I don't want Tae to die either."

"He's dyin', already, Terrell. Look at 'im."

Terrell saw that Shawntae's eyes had again rolled back to the whites. He punctuated his wheezing with incoherent moans and his body trembled worse than before.

The revolver returned to Brock's hand. "We gotta do it, man."

Terrell stared at Brock holding the gun. Brock leveled the firearm, staring back at Terrell with eyes that seemed to beg him not to try anything stupid. Terrell returned his gaze to what was left of Shawntae.

"Go on," Terrell agreed, in a broken voice. "Do it."

"Leave it up to me, huh?" Brock hissed, keeping the gun pointed at Terrell. "Naw, that ain't the move. This time you gon' really hafta gitcha hands dirty."

"What the fuck are you sayin'?" Terrell shrieked. The park lights returned, illuminating his living nightmare once more.

Brock aimed the gun at his cousin's chest, holding it with both hands. "I'm sayin' you got too much on me, cuz. I don't wanna have to kill you, too - but the only way I kin let you live is if I know I got somethin' on you like you got all this shit on me."

"You can't be askin' me to kill him," Terrell protested, trying to ignore the sounds of Shawntae's struggling breaths.

Brock's voice grew tremulous. "I'm askin' you to make a decision, cuz. Do I lose one a the niggas I love most tonight or do I lose 'em both?"

Terrell stood silent for a few moments, as the park lights gave way to darkness once more. "You muthafucka," he growled. "You've turned into a real piece of shit, Brock."

"I know that," Brock said, nodding. "I know that. I hate this!" He took his left hand off the gun and waved it about. "But iss how iss gotta be. Now what's it gonna be?"

Terrell looked down at Shawntae. The big man's eyes stretched wide with shock. Blood continued to flee his wound. Crimson spittle and specks of gore trailed from his quivering, groaning mouth.

"I got nothin' to do it wit," Terrell grumbled, looking at the gun.

"Git a rock from ova there." Brock pointed to a grassy knoll just beyond the underpass and just off the bike trail. "Make sure iss a big one. You don't wanna have to hit 'im twice."

"How kin you be so cold, man?" Terrell cried. "You want me to bash his head in? He won't even be able to have an open casket."

Brock shook his head. "He ain't gon' have a casket at all. We gon' put him somewhere he can't be found."

"What?" Terrell said, his eyes grown huge. "We can't do that! He's like our brother, Brock!"

"Yeah, jus' like I'm like your brova. We're all like brovas- right? That ain't stop you from tryna beat the livin' shit outta me, though. If you hadn't been wylin', I neva even woulda pulled the fuckin' gun out! Now, you betta git a rock or a brick or somethin' 'n' put him outta his misery before I put you outta yours!"

Brock followed behind Terrell as they walked to the knoll.

"You try anything slick 'n' I'll shoot you, cuz," he snarled through clenched teeth that were as red as if someone had painted them. "I swear to God, I'll put one in you. I don't want to, but I'll do it."

Moments later, Terrell walked towards Shawntae, holding a brick sized rock in his right hand. "N-no," Tae gasped, his dilated eyes managing to focus on Terrell as more spittle escaped his mouth and more blood gushed from his abdominal region.

"I'm sorry, Tae," Terrell moaned. His vision clouded with tears as he raised the big rock overhead. His entire torso traveled downward with his swing, mustering a mighty blow that smashed Shawntae's skull. The park lights shone brightest at that moment, as if someone had pressed the flash on a giant camera and captured Terrell's hideous deed for all posterity. The fallen peacemaker convulsed twice before falling still.

V

Brock attempted to comfort Terrell, speaking in a tone that bordered on paternal. "I know that was terrible for you, but we'd betta git that body into my trunk right now 'n' git him outta here. It'd be just our luck if a cop decided to check the park out right now. Shit, I'd just shoot it out wit' the dude if that happened. Betta to go that way than take the slow death from the state."

The deserted park had fallen into darkness again. Terrell looked around, almost wishing that a police cruiser would come by and bring this ordeal to a turbulent end. He couldn't deny that rotting in prison was a suitable punishment for him. First he had allowed those girls to die. Now he had murdered Shawntae. The fact that he had been forced to do the latter did nothing for his conscience. Neither did the certainty that Brock would have killed him and finished Tae if he had refused.

"Yo, snap out of that shit!" Brock's growl jarred Terrell from his reverie. His right hand kept the gun trained on Terrell as he used his left hand to fish out his car keys.

"Open the trunk and force him into it," Brock ordered, tossing the keys. "I know you're strong enough to do it from the way you were kickin' my ass."

Terrell bent at the waist after completing the strenuous task. His hands rested just above his knees. Tae's blood coated him as he struggled to catch his breath, trembling as if he had Parkinson's Disease.

"Throw that rock in the trunk," Brock said, waving at the object that had finished Shawntae off with his gun. "We'll be gittin' rid of that."

Terrell did as told before turning to his cousin for further instructions.

"Take off that bloody tee shirt," Brock said.

Terrell wasted no time in stripping down to a white cotton tank top.

"Wipe your hands off 'n' throw that shit in the trunk."

Once that direction was followed, Brock told his cousin to lie down on the ground, stomach first.

"I ain't doin' that Brock," Terrell's voice quavered. "I ain't gonna die laid out on the ground like some dog. You wanna shoot me, you'll have to do it face to face."

Tears streamed down Brock's face as he shook his head. The park lights shone on him as he used his free hand to wipe them away. "You think I would do you like that? You my cousin, man. I love you. I just wanna make sure you don't try nothin' while I take off my tee shirt. Iss got blood on it, too. I know your mind ain't right, right now- so I don't wanna give you a chance to do somethin' stupid so I'll have to shoot you. Got damn, cousin. I can't believe you thought I would do you like that."

Terrell didn't know what to make of what his cousin had just said. He decided to do as he was told, praying that Brock was telling the truth, knowing that he was a dead man if Brock wasn't. His trembling worsened as he lay helpless on the asphalt. A puddle of Shawntae's blood marred the ground a few inches from his face. He felt a terrible welling within his bowels. He had heard about people shitting on themselves if they were scared enough, but he never imagined himself on the verge of it.

"Aight, git up," Brock commanded after what seemed like an eternity. The contents of Terrell's bowels shifted inward.

Terrell saw that his cousin was now stripped down to a wife beater like his own. Brock had wiped the blood away from where Terrell had pummeled him. The strawberry on his left cheek had swelled to a nice size. He managed to keep the revolver pointed at Terrell even as he closed the trunk. The trunk had been cleared of outward traces of Tae's blood.

Brock nodded toward the car. "Pick up the keys and drive, nigga. I'll tell you where to go. 'N' don't try to do nothin' stupid or I'll shoot you. Tha's how it got to be until this shit is ova. You do somethin' stupid 'n' I'll shoot you. Cooperate 'n' you git to go home in one piece. Please don't make me shoot you, Terrell. I'm already fucked up over Tae. Please don't make me have to take you out."

Brock prattled without end as Terrell drove, speaking of how haunted he was about killing the girls, maintaining that none of this would have happened if "that bitch" Tia hadn't attacked him. He swore that he had only shot Mr. Johnson to protect all three of them. He cursed Terrell, saying that Terrell should have trusted him instead of confronting him the way Terrell had. He swore that he had only pulled the gun because he was scared. He just wanted Terrell to back off. Tae should have never tried to take the gun from him.

Terrell couldn't tell if Brock was trying to convince Terrell or himself. Nor did he care. The only thing that mattered was that Tae had died tonight and Terrell might soon join him.

"I would've neva used it on y'all," Brock said, switching the gun to his left hand and pointing it at Terrell's side. "Turn left."

Terrell spoke for the first time since telling Brock he'd have to shoot him face to face, having realized something about the route they were traveling. "We goin' to your house?"

"Yeah. I gotta git a shovel from Uncle Ramon's shed."

"Well, then- why'd you have me drive all around the mulberry bush?"

Brock smiled. "There you go- not trustin' me again." He took a deep breath. "I didn't want to come straight out here. What if somebody was followin' us?"

Terrell suppressed his urge to protest, submitting himself to the acceptance of his cousin's complete paranoia. But, then- what was the expression? Just because you're paranoid doesn't mean no one's out to get you? Yeah, that sounded about right.

Besides, maybe Brock wasn't the only one coming apart at the seams. Terrell wondered what had gotten hold of him earlier. It was as if he had been possessed. Even the threat of Brock's gun did not stop him. Tae had to get shot for his sanity to return. Tae had died because of his loss of control. That burden already felt far heavier than his complicity in the deaths of those girls.

Shawntae was- had been like family. The big man had been more brother than friend. They had all been like brothers before that horrible night at Terrell's apartment.

"Pull up in the alley," Brock commanded, interrupting Terrell's train of thought. "You need to git your shit together, too. You kin do all the cryin', drinkin', or shoot some fuckin' dope if you want to, once we bury him. Right now, we gotta keep our shit together. Tae wouldn't want us to git caught."

"You muthafucka," Terrell growled, glaring at his cousin as he stopped the car in the directed spot.

Brock shrugged. "Iss true. I am a muthafucka. Maybe I'm one of the worst niggas around, after the shit I've done. Now, hop ova that fence 'n' git the shovel outta the shed. My triflin' uncle neva locks it. Be quiet about it, too."

Shovel in hand, Terrell returned to the car, pondering making a run for it before deciding that he just didn't have enough spirit left in him. He heard the clicking sound of the trunk unlocking as Brock motioned for him to place the shovel there. Terrell looked away as he dropped it in, not wanting to cast his eyes upon his dead friend.

Terrell returned behind the wheel and listened to further driving directions. This time Brock did not bemoan the horrible things that had happened. He spoke only to indicate when Terrell should turn. It was as if what he'd said on the way to getting the shovel had cleared his conscience. The notion that doing so was so easy for Brock ignited fresh terror within Terrell. Brock noticed his cousin's alarm and instructed him to pull over.

"You kin stop all that sweatin' 'n' breathin' hard, cuz," he spoke over the idling engine. "I swear I ain't gon' do nothin' to you."

Terrell barely managed to croak a response. "Aight."

"Terrell- I swear to you, cousin," Brock pleaded, tears welling once more. "I'm not gon' do nothin' to you as long as you don't try nothin'. You gon' try anything?"

Terrell shook his head.

"Aight, then. I'm not gon' hurt you. I still love you, cuz. I'm sorry about erythang tha's happened."

Brock switched the gun to his right hand, placing his left on Terrell's shoulder.

"Just chill right here 'til you're ready ta drive again, cuz. Just chill right here."

Tears streaked down both of their faces as the Cutlass idled at the curb. The tears fell for their slain friend, for all of the horrible things that had happened and for what they had become.

VI

After crying a bucket of tears, Terrell composed himself enough to continue the drive. Their trip terminated at an industrial park in eastern Baltimore County, near the junction of Essex and Middle River. A large field overlooked the cluster of nondescript buildings, its' foot resting about fifty yards beyond the rearmost of them. As instructed, Terrell parked the Cutlass at the edge of it. He wondered how Brock even knew about such a place. Had he been scouting for places to dump a body? Why would he do that unless he hadn't intended to stop killing with Mr. Johnson?

Maybe Tae wasn't the only one whom Brock intended to place in the ground. Maybe he intended to tie up all loose ends at once by having Terrell dig his own grave. No, Brock had to realize what kind of heat would come from the cops if both he and Tae disappeared. The big man's disappearance would cast enough suspicion by its' lonesome. Brock had to know that killing Terrell wasn't in his best interests. On the other hand, his paranoid mind might have convinced him of the opposite. Whatever the case, Terrell decided to play his part to the bitter end. His broken spirit strangled any possible notion of heroics.

However he had become acquainted with the industrial park, Brock had chosen well. It was as secluded from the main road as it was deserted. It was a great place to dispose of a body.

Brock continued to use the threat of the gun to maintain control. He ordered Terrell to drag Shawntae's corpse out of the trunk, up to the hilly crest of the field.

Terrell ran on fumes by the time he managed to haul the heavy body to the high mound where Brock instructed. His lungs burned, joining muscles he didn't know he had in their misery. Terrell gauged that he had dragged Shawntae's corpse at least thirty yards. Before being stuck with the task of maneuvering his dead body, Terrell had thought that Shawntae weighed maybe 240. He now thought that to be a gross underestimate.

A crescent moon fed the field its only light. Brock fell in close to Terrell, gun still pointed. He used his left hand to toss the shovel at his cousin's feet.

"Rest up good, cuz," Brock said. "When you gitcha self together, you're gonna dig the hole."

"Why don't you… dig it…yourself?" Terrell gasped. "You're makin' me do everything."

Brock chuckled. "See, I would like to help you, cuz. But I think you're jus' crazy enough to try somethin' if you had the chance."

"Fuck you."

"Fuck you, Terrell. You should be thankful I'm lookin' out for you. I'm doin' erythang I kin not to hafta kill you."

After catching his breath, Terrell set about the grueling task of burying Shawntae. He pushed his already overtaxed muscles past empty, groaning as lactic acid stung him. Only stark terror of Brock kept Terrell from collapsing in a combination of guilt and physical misery after each bend of his waist, each push of the shovel into the earth, each soil-clearing swing of the shoulders. His actions had caused Shawntae to be shot and he had finished the man off himself. Gunpoint or not, he had chosen to take his friend's life. He now prepared a secret grave for the man, a grave that might never be discovered. Only he and Brock would know for sure what had happened to Shawntae, unless Terrell went to the authorities. Terrell couldn't envision any way to do that without fucking himself over for life.

As terrible as he felt about everything that had happened, Terrell's life still meant something to him. Hell, it meant more to him than Tae's. That's why he had done what he'd done. It wasn't like Tae could have survived losing all of that blood, anyway. *You don't know that for sure*, he chastised himself. *You had a chance to try to get the gun from Brock, but instead you froze, like a fucking coward. You don't deserve any better than what 'Tae got.*

Whether he deserved to or not, Terrell didn't want to die. He didn't want to rot in prison either. So he'd do as Brock said and keep his fucking mouth shut about it afterward. He'd keep his mouth shut and try to find a way to live with himself.

The burning in Terrell's muscles subsided just enough for him to fight through the summer heat which assaulted his body even at this late hour. He grunted as he worked, tuning out the occasional comments that his gun-toting cousin made. After what seemed like forever, the hole grew large enough.

Brock found the audacity to pat Terrell on the back. "Good job, cuz. Now all you got to do is dump 'im in."

Although he didn't say so out loud, Terrell objected to that phrasing. He was not going to dump Shawntae anywhere. Instead, he placed his fallen friend into the earthen tomb with great care.

"I'm sorry, Tae." Terrell hugged the broken corpse. "I'm so sorry."

"I'm sorry too, big fella," Brock sniffled. Terrell saw that he was in tears again. He marveled that his cousin could do such horrible things despite feeling terrible about them. He supposed that he wasn't much better.

"You gotta cova him up now, cuz," Brock said. "I know you're dead tired, but I can't do it for you, cuz I still think you're crazy enough to make a move. Take your time, though. You don't have to hurry. Nobody's comin'."

Brock's supportiveness made Terrell want to vomit. It made him want to pummel Brock into a bloody pulp. But he couldn't do anything because Brock still held the gun. The only thing Terrell would accomplish if he tried anything was getting killed and buried, right along with Shawntae. As he covered Tae's burial spot, some morbid part of him wished that his cousin would go ahead and pull the trigger.

VI

"So what happens, now?" Terrell asked, the grisly task now done. He walked back to Brock's car, shovel in hand. Brock followed close behind him. Terrell didn't have to turn to know that the gun remained pointed at him.

"You drive back to your crib 'n' I'll take the car from there," Brock replied in a calm tone. "I'ma go back to the park and scrub the blood off the ground best as I kin. I'ma burn those tee shirts and clean the blood 'n' shit out of this car, too. I'll make sure the rock and the gun are neva found eitha. Got to git rid of as much evidence as possible. You feel me?"

"Naw, man," Terrell dissented, shaking his head. "I'm goin' to Mo's. I don't wanna be alone tonight."

"You can't do that, man," Brock said. "Look at you. You look like you just buried somebody. Smell like it, too."

Terrell inspected himself. Granules of dirt and sweat stained his tank top. Sweat also coated his body. "I did just bury somebody."

"You know what I mean, cuz."

"Fine. Take me back to my crib so I can shower, then take me over there."

Brock's eyes widened. "Tha's a lot a extra time, cuz."

"You can't do that for me?" Terrell howled. "You can't do that for me after the shit you just made me do?"

"Aight," Brock relented. "Aight. Jus' make sure iss a quick shower." He motioned toward the trunk with his free hand. "Put the shovel in the trunk 'n' let's git out of here."

Terrell emerged from his apartment about 40 minutes later, having changed into a fresh tee shirt and a fresh pair of jean shorts. Gauze covered his scraped palms.

"Feel better now?" Brock asked. The gun was nowhere to be seen.

"I feel cleaner. Physically cleaner, anyway."

Brock backed out of his parking space and started toward Monet's place. "You ain't gon' tell her nothin' about this- are you?"

"Why would I tell her somethin' about this? So she kin know I killed somebody?"

Brock laughed. "When you put it like that, I feel real stupid for askin'."

Fifteen minutes later, Terrell exited Brock's car in front of the townhouse Monet rented with her roommate. Brock already knew where she lived, having picked Terrell up from there or dropped him off a number of times before he became someone to fear. Otherwise, Terrell would never have come there in the lunatic's company.

"It'll be aight, cuz," Brock said. "You'll see." He shifted the Cutlass Supreme into reverse and backed out of his parking space. The vehicle's huge taillights illuminated the cul-de-sac for a few moments, fading away as Brock drove into the night.

"Yeah, fuck you- it'll be aight," Terrell muttered. He took time to gather his thoughts before ringing Monet's doorbell. He thought long and hard of a lie to explain his whereabouts and gauze covered palms, but he just couldn't invent one.

Terrell sat on Monet's steps, wondering how long it would be before his cousin's paranoia led him to change his mind about not wanting to hurt Terrell- the same way Brock had changed his mind about whether Mr. Johnson had seen anything that night. A parade of other terrible thoughts marched in step with that one.

Alone in the dark for what seemed like forever, Terrell decided to tell Monet the truth, consequences be damned.

# Chapter Six

I

Violent knocking stirred Monet from her bedroom. The alarm clock on her nightstand revealed that it was 3:26 a.m., but worrying about Terrell had kept her awake. She rushed toward the front door, running into her roommate Carletta in the hall. Both young women were dressed in robes.

"Who the hell has lost their got damn mind this time of night?" Carletta grumbled.

"I don't know," Monet answered, hoping that it was Terrell and that he was alright. She beat Carletta to the door, looking through the peephole. Her first hope was granted, but Terrell looked a long way from alright. He wore different clothes than he had earlier and his shoulders bowed as if they bore a great weight.

Monet flicked on the porch light and opened the front door. She saw that the facial expression Terrell wore matched his miserable posture. Gauze covered both of his palms, just beneath his thumbs. She took hold of his hands and examined them, seeing that tiny scratches trailed up each palm. She hugged him. "Terrell, baby," her voice cracked. "What happened to you?"

Carletta gave Terrell a once over before grumbling, "I'm going back to bed."

"I gotta talk to you," Terrell said. He avoided eye contact as he spoke.

"Well come on in here and talk, baby," Monet spoke in a soothing tone, placing her hands on his shoulders. "Tell me what's wrong."

"Naw," he said, pulling away. "Not in there. Le's talk in your car. Okay?"

"Okay," she agreed, wondering what could cause him to be so wild-eyed and jumpy. "Okay. Just let me throw something on."

Terrell climbed into the passenger seat when Monet returned. A tortured expression affixed his face as he stared into Monet's eyes. She returned his stare, waiting for him to speak.

A long silence passed before he managed, "I don't deserve you, Mo. I don't deserve you at all."

"Sure you do," she said, kissing him on the cheek. "You're a great guy."

He shook his head. "No, I ain't. You're jus' sayin' that because you don't know."

Monet's eyes widened. "What is it that I don't know, Terrell?"

"When you were in Virginia Beach, I cheated on you."

Her eyebrows furrowed. "Is that your idea of a joke?"

"No. It happened the Friday you left. You weren't even gone a whole day 'n' I fucked some raunchy bitch. I didn't mean to. I was supposed to just talk to the chick. Brock 'n' Shanwtae came through with some girls 'n' I was supposed to jus' talk to the chick while they tried to get at the ones they were with. But I got so fuckin' drunk 'n' the chick started makin' moves on me. She was sexy, too."

Monet slapped him hard enough to leave a handprint on his cheek. He bore it without complaint.

"What the fuck is wrong with you?" She screamed. "You come here looking all fucked up- to tell me that? Why'd you have to tell me that?"

"Shh!" Terrell pleaded, placing his left index finger to his lips. "You gon' make a scene, baby. It's quiet around here."

"I don't give a fuck how it is around here!" She cocked back to slap him again.

"Go ahead," Terrell said. "It's the least I deserve." He laughed. "Shit, I deserve for you to use your fists."

Monet resisted her violent compulsion, trembling as she spoke. "No, I'm going back inside. I'm sure I'll spend the rest of the night crying. I hope I don't shed any more tears over you after that. You have a nice life, Terrell."

He grabbed her wrist. "Not yet," he said. "You have to hear the rest first."

Monet yanked her arm free. "You want me to listen to more of that shit?"

"I need you to." Terrell's lips trembled as fresh tears streamed down his face. "There's nobody else, Mo. If you never wanna talk me to after this, I'll jus' have to accept it. I know that's only right. But, I need you to listen to me now. *Please.*"

"I can't believe you!" Monet howled. "You want me to listen to more of how you fucked some bitch? News flash, Terrell- you didn't have to tell me!"

Terrell's anguish didn't prevent him from recognizing the disgust in Monet's eyes. He knew that he deserved for her to storm off and never speak to him again. He deserved for her to hate every fiber of his being and far worse. Yet, she remained in the car.

"I know how incredibly horny 20 year old guys are and you never promised me that you wouldn't fuck anyone else," She said, pointing an index finger at his face. "I would have just hoped that you would use protection and not bring it in my face. But here you are- bringing it in my face! Why? Because you feel guilty? If so, you should've just learned to live with that shit. I know you're not stupid enough to think anything good would come of telling me. Maybe you just didn't want to deal with me anymore. If so, you sure picked a coward's way of ending it. And you have the nerve to cry? I'm the one who should be crying."

The dam burst on that cue, Monet's chest heaving with sobs as she rested her head on the steering wheel. Terrell once again learned the lesson that no matter how bad he felt at a particular moment, he could always feel worse in the next. He had done the damage that reduced Monet to this state. As much as it pained him, he had more misery to give her.

Terrell had done enough of his own crying to know that the tears had to stop at some point. He waited for as long as it took Monet to regain her composure. He rested a timid hand on her shoulder when she did.

"I'm sorry, Mo," he said. "I'm so sorry."

"Yeah, sure." Her words were shaky. "Did you at least use a condom? Did you at least do that?"

"Yeah."

"Well, that's nice." She smirked. "Safe sex and all that good stuff. A man should practice safe sex when he's fucking around on his girlfriend!" She wiped her eyes and nose on her tee shirt, blowing snot into the collar.

A wan smile accompanied her voice as it grew calm. “Not very lady like- I know”.

Terrell squeezed the shoulder his hand rested on. “You’ll always be a lady to me.”

“Don’t,” she protested.

“Don’t what?”

She pushed his hand away. “Don’t be nice to me. And don’t comfort me. How can you comfort me when you’re the one who’s hurt me? What kind of sick shit is that? Are you toying with me?”

Terrell hung his head. “Never,” he said. “Never. I would never toy with you. I’m so ashamed to hurt you like this. I wish I could take it all back.”

An interminable amount of passed before Terrell found the courage to seek eye contact. “Listen- jus’ let me hurry up and finish what I have to say, please. Then we kin be done with each other. Like I said before, I don’t deserve you. Not at all. I guess I don’t deserve anything good in life, now.”

“Cut the pity party,” Monet hissed. Her eyes smoldered as she jabbed a finger at him. “Go ahead and say what you have to say, Terrell. I don’t know what more there could be, but go ahead and say what you have to say.”

II

Though she remained silent as Terrell told the tale, Monet’s eyes confessed her every emotion. The first mention of murder deflated every iota of righteous fury she’d felt toward him, causing a chill to travel up her spine. Terrell felt a chill as well, because recounting the horrible night that led him here caused him to relive it.

Monet's eyes widened as the account unfolded. By the time Terrell detailed Shawntae being shot, her pupils looked like they could have been dilated from drug use. The brown wells revealed that she didn't want to believe everything he had told her. They also revealed that she knew every horrible bit of it was true.

When Terrell told of bashing Shawntae's head in with a rock, Monet gasped like a small child awakening from a terrible nightmare to realize they're alone in the dark. She followed the gasp with sobbing. Terrell pulled her close, feeling a fresh tide of guilt for reducing her to this state. He thought that his grisly story would change her view of the world forever.

He knew that it was selfish to burden her with such horrible knowledge. But he also knew that if Monet loved him enough to bear the entire horrid tale she also loved him enough to help him- and he needed her help. She trembled against him as he waited for an indication that hearing more wouldn't overwhelm her.

Her voice was more sigh than speech when she broke the silence. "What did you do with Tae?"

Terrell took a deep breath. "We buried him. I buried him. Brock forced me to do it. Kept the gun pointed at me the whole time."

"Oh, my God." Monet straightened up, caressing his cheek. Her eyes were mournful. "He could have killed you anytime he felt like it."

"I gotta piss," Terrell groaned, feeling as if his bladder were about to explode.

"Go ahead." Monet motioned toward her front door. "I didn't lock it. I'll be right here."

As soon as Terrell returned to the car, Monet said, "You need my help- don't you?" Disgust, worry, and resignation shared the canvas of her face.

He nodded. "I'm gonna git out of town- go visit Malik until I kin figure out what else to do. I need you to help me git away from here."

"Okay," Monet said, sighing. She reached across him and placed her trembling hands over his knuckles, kneading them with her thumbs. "Okay."

III

Brock assaulted his car with water from a garden hose, not caring that it was past five in the morning. Nor did he care that anyone who saw what he was up to in the rear of his grandmother's house might wonder if he had gone crazy. If he had gone crazy, he was crazy as a fox and too sly to get caught. He would not be caught, no matter what.

That's why he'd shot Mr. Johnson after spending countless time obsessing over the possibility that the old dude might have seen Tia sitting on that couch. He just couldn't take a chance on whether or not the guy had seen anything, on whether or not the cops would get to him someday.

He hadn't dared to tell Terrell and Shawntae of his plans, not after the way they responded to his suggestion that the girls' brother be eliminated. He still had a tiny suspicion that Wendell might have set the cops on him, but even if Wendell had the cops didn't have enough to make it stick or he'd be locked up already. So Brock had let the poor guy live.

Mr. Johnson had to go, though. He had to be got. Brock just couldn't stand spending every day wondering whether or not that old head could confirm that he had been with one of the murdered girls.

Brock continued to spray his car as his mind replayed the aftermath of Tae's death. After leaving Terrell, he'd driven back to his house, maintaining a nice even speed. He didn't need any cops pulling him over while he looked as if he had just been in a scrape and still had some of Tae's blood in his trunk. He moved with stealth to keep from awakening his grandmother, soaping up some rags and tossing them into a bucket. He drove his cleaning tools back to the scene of Shawntae's demise and soaped every visible speck of blood from the ground. When the park lights grew dark, he used a flashlight he had brought along to light the way.

Once he completed the task of cleaning Shawntae's blood from the scene, Brock wiped down the gun and the rock that had brought the big man to an end. He drove over to the Hanover Street Bridge and pulled over on the bridge's shoulder, checking to see that no other motorists passed by before pitching the weapons into the Patapsco River. Once that task was done, he returned to the same part of Herring Run Park where he and the others had dismembered the three girls' bodies. He set fire to the bloody tee shirts at the stream's edge, watching them burn with a heavy mind. When they were charred to his satisfaction, he kicked the black remains into the stream.

His next task was driving the Cutlass to the Self-Cleaning Car Wash at the bottom of Moravia Road. The gas station that housed it stood deserted at that time of morning, just as Brock had hoped. He used a strong cleaning solution and thick rags to scrub down his upholstery and trunk. He then ran the token operated vacuum hose through three cycles in an effort to get rid of any dirt that he and Terrell had tracked in from the field where Tae had been buried.

*It ain't sposed to be like this*, Brock thought. He wasn't supposed to have to threaten Terrell at gunpoint, forcing him to do his bidding. Shawntae wasn't supposed to die.

Brock didn't regret having shot Mr. Johnson. He felt that doing so had been necessary for all of their protection. He just wished Terrell hadn't figured it out.

He had tried to make it look like a random robbery. *Shit, plenty of people get shot in robberies*, he thought, *especially in Baltimore fuckin' city! Half the people who do robberies in Baltimore City are geeked up junkies. Niggas like that'll kill just if they think somebody made a wrong move. It was supposed to look like the dude got killed by somebody like that. That's why I took his fuckin' wallet. Is Terrell really that fuckin' smart- to figure it out as soon as it happened?*

*The nigga's always been smart about books and shit like that,* Brock thought. *But this shit is different. How the fuck could he figure that shit out so quickly?*

He decided that it had to be because Terrell had thought the worst of him ever since he'd killed those girls.

*Maybe I deserve to be thought of that way*, Brock thought. He had killed four people and caused the death of a fifth- the death of someone who was like a brother to him. No- that wasn't all his fault.

How was Brock supposed to know that Terrell would figure things out so quickly and that he would react so violently after he did? He would never forget the wild look in his cousin's eyes when he attacked him. Terrell had looked as if he wanted to kill Brock.

He'd pulled the gun just to back Terrell off. After that, things got out of control. Brock tried not to dwell on the tragic outcome of that confrontation, but his mind was like a faucet that someone had ripped the head from. He continued to rinse the car as he agonized, although it couldn't get any cleaner than its' present state.

Brock told himself that he'd have years to shed tears and drink to Tae's memory. But first, he had to figure out how to make sure he didn't go down for the crimes he'd committed, for the terrible things he'd done. He knew that it would be like Death Row Monopoly if he was ever caught and convicted. Do not pass go, go straight to lethal injection.

Brock couldn't see himself ending up like that. He told himself that Tae wouldn't have wanted that. Tae would have wanted him to move on with his life. Tae had always been that way, wanting everything to work out for everyone.

The big man had always been the peacemaker of their group, squashing countless conflicts between Brock and Terrell over the years. It was a damn shame that he'd died behind trying to end such a conflict. Why'd he have to grab the fucking gun? Brock had no intention of using it. He just wanted Terrell to stay the fuck away from him.

Brock shrugged. What's done was done and now Tae wasn't around to squash the biggest conflict the two cousins ever had. Brock didn't trust Terrell any more than Terrell trusted him. He hated the way Terrell had been acting ever since the night with those girls. No, hate wasn't the right word.

Fear was what Brock felt. He feared the way Terrell acted as if he thought he had suffered the most, even though he hadn't had to dirty his hands at all before tonight. He'd been avoiding Brock and Tae like the plague, like he was better than them or as if maybe they just disgusted him.

With everything that had happened tonight, there was even more weight for Terrell to carry. Brock felt afraid that college boy couldn't handle it. He had forced Terrell to finish Shawntae off so that Terrell would have blood on his own hands, thinking that would guarantee Terrell's silence. In the aftermath, Brock realized that what happened didn't guarantee that his cousin would keep quiet. It was still possible that Terrell might snitch to try to give himself a clear conscience, not giving a fuck about how much prison time he'd have to do.

Brock did not doubt that Terrell might be able to get some kind of sweetheart's deal from the cops while the only thing Brock got was a dose of lethal poison in his veins. In a dark alley that was silent save for the occasional scurrying rat and the pattering of water against his car, Brock considered the notion that letting Terrell live might be too much of a risk.

Could he really kill his cousin? Had he become that cold- that ruthless? If so, was there a way for him to do it without drawing more heat from the cops? The only thing Brock felt sure about was his determination to do everything in his power to keep from being caught. He would not be caught, no matter what he had to do.

IV

Monet felt obligated to help Terrell reach safety before confronting her feelings about his infidelity. *There's no point in being angry with a dead man,* she thought. Besides, *cheating on me isn't a crime worthy of death. It's worth a serious ass kicking maybe, but not death.*

Her cellular phone display read 4:39 a.m. as she exited her car in front of his apartment building. Empty cars parked in their spaces were her only company. The dead stillness gave Monet a chill. Her newfound fear of Brock caused her to scan the perimeter. She thought him capable of lying in wait for Terrell.

Monet pulled a can of mace from her purse. She held Terrell's keys in her other hand. She chuckled, musing that she only carried the mace because her father insisted. She'd never imagined that she would have occasion to use it. She'd always thought that he worried too much when he insisted that anything could happen in a rough city like Baltimore. He had an apology coming if she made it through this ordeal in one piece.

Monet felt grateful for the dim light an overhanging bulb provided as she ventured into the hallway of Terrell's building. She shivered, despite the fact that it was still warm in the wee hours. She let herself into Terrell's apartment, flicking the light switch in his living room on. She kept the mace can in a ready position as she turned on all the other lights within.

Monet breathed a little easier after confirming that she was alone. She tried not to think about the fact that three girls had been killed here. She also tried not to think about how many times she'd showered in the very tub where a girl had been killed.

Terrell's backpack lay in a corner of his bedroom, in front of his decrepit plastic hamper. Monet hurried, stuffing the backpack with several changes of clothes and underwear. After that was done, the large bag still had plenty of room for snacks that she would insist Terrell take on his trip. She finished packing by placing his necessary toiletries in a small front flap. She turned out the lights and exited with the urgency of Lot fleeing Sodom.

Pack on her back like a young schoolgirl, Monet periscoped the parking lot, just as she had on her way in. Relieved to find it still deserted, she lowered the mace can and got into the car.

V

Joe's Motel, a seedy little establishment at the junction of North Avenue and Howard Street, rented rooms for $29.95 a night. Those who rented them got what they paid for. Terrell's room was typical of the accommodations.

An uncarpeted floor of faltering plywood promised ass splinters for anyone stupid enough to sit on it, foot splinters for those asinine enough to walk across it barefoot. The tiny shower seemed appropriate for a state prison, as did the lidless metal toilet. Barely an arm's length of space separated the toilet and ancient sink.

As he lay on cheap, itchy sheets and a mattress that looked like it should have been tossed sometime during the Industrial Age, Terrell thought of all that had happened that night and how he should proceed next.

Terrell had used Monet's cellular to call Malik after she agreed to help him, concocting a lie to explain why he was calling at such a crazy hour. Well, it wasn't a total lie. He and Monet did have some very serious problems now and he did wonder if things would work out. It was also true that he wanted to go to New York to clear his head. He only omitted the parts about his involvement in five people meeting their violent ends.

Malik accepted what Terrell told him at face value and invited him up, saying that he would be glad to meet at Port Authority the following day after work. Monet then took Terrell to an ATM (where he cleaned out all of his money save for $3 that couldn't be rounded off with the transaction) and brought him to the dirt bag motel that he now waited in.

Anxiety tormented Terrell as he waited for Monet's return, visualizing a nightmare scenario of Brock lying in wait for him outside of his apartment, then deciding to kidnap her when she showed up in his stead. Try as he might, he couldn't convince himself that he was being paranoid. A rickety ceiling fan provided little cool in his shit hole of a room, but he would have been sweating even if it were the dead of winter. He wished he had some stiff liquor to drink.

Unable to stand the suspense any longer, Terrell labored to dial the rotary phone that sat on the room's shoddy nightstand. He felt relieved when the call trudged through and Monet answered her cell phone.

"Is e-evrything okay?" Terrell stammered.

"Yes. I'm on my way back to you, now. I have everything that you need."

*I'm on my way back to you, now.* Terrell felt bittersweet to hear Monet speak those words. Not simply, "I'm on my way back." She was on her way back to him, maybe for the last time.

If it was the last time, Terrell intended to make it memorable. Concerning the last words she'd said, she didn't have everything he needed. He needed a way out, but he wasn't sure there was one.

Terrell pounced on Monet as soon as she entered the room, kissing and caressing her in all the right places. She returned his passion with her own before breaking away. Neither of them paid heed to the shoddy mattress and bedclothes as they enjoyed each other for what might prove to be the last time.

VI

Terrell slept like a newborn, despite the uncomfortable bed. He would have easily missed the eleven a.m. checkout time if Monet hadn't awakened him. He passed on the hideous shower, opting to dry wash in front of the sink. Monet gave him fresh band-aids for the scrapes on his hands. He declined an offer to shower at her place, insisting that he had to get going as soon as possible.

"Alright." She kissed him on the cheek. "But I want you to clean up real good once you meet up with Malik."

Terrell flashed his most charming smile. "Will do, Nurse Mo."

She dropped him off at the Travel Plaza a short time later. He lingered with her in the parking lot, not wanting to separate from her, wondering if he would ever get a chance to be with her again. They held hands for a long time, enjoying each other's silence as buses debarked and embarked.

"You'd better go," Monet said, her eyes moist. "I'll pray for you."

"Thanks." Terrell pecked her on the cheek. "I need your prayers. I need your prayers and a lot more."

Monet leaned across her seat and drew him into her arms, hugging him as if she meant to squeeze all the breath from his body. Tears flowed unencumbered as she released him, her lips trembling. "Oh God, Terrell. Oh, God. I hope you'll be okay."

Terrell wiped some of her tears away, but more fell to take their place. He smiled and tried to seem strong. "I still got a chance of comin' out of this okay, Mo," he spoke in what he hoped was a confident tone, desperate to convince someone of the truth in that statement.

# Chapter Seven

I

Terrell breathed a sigh of relief as he walked off the Greyhound bus and into Port Authority. After using a pay phone to announce his arrival, he waited for his host to arrive. He snacked on some Cheetos that he'd bought from a newsstand when Malik approached him.

"Wassup, Baltimore?" Malik said, wearing a broad grin. The blooming afro that had sat atop his head when he left Baltimore was now styled into fresh twists. Tall and sinewy, he was dressed in a sharp shirt and tie with slacks.

"Ain't nothin'," Terrell answered, pounding fists with Malik. "Shit, you look like GQ magazine."

Malik laughed and popped the collar on his shirt. "Oh, this? Just work clothes, you know. A brother's got to look the part." He sniffed at Terrell. "Is that you smellin' like that? Got damn, that is you. Shit man, you smell like you've been sleepin' outside. What the hell? You didn't shower before you left? I know Monet's all 'at (his New York accent transformed all into *oll)* and everything but don't let no shorty have you broke down like that."

Terrell frowned. "Ain't nobody breakin' me down, man. The hot water wasn't workin' in the apartment this morning. You know I wasn't gonna freeze my balls off tryna git super clean."

"Yeah?" Malik started up the steps that led to the street. "I hate it when that happens. Those cheap bastards at Parkview Gardens act like it's so hard to keep hot water running. Come on, man." He pointed at Terrell's backpack.

"I see you traveled light, huh? That's cool. I'ma take you back to the crib- get your funky ass cleaned up before we get into anything."

They changed trains twice during Terrell's first trip on the New York City subway.

"This is my hood," Malik said, gesturing after they exited at their final stop. He and Terrell walked past an endless sea of brick houses and storefronts. "It ain't so bad- right?"

Scanning the surroundings, Terrell found them to look much like the less blighted neighborhoods back home. Little kids played ball games in the street while teenagers stood around, talking loud, dressed like extras for the latest rap video. An old woman pushed a shopping cart past a corner store. "Naw. It ain't so bad."

"Shit, I'm glad you came," Malik said, clapping Terrell on the shoulder. "I wish you would've come for the Fourth, though. I could've really showed you some shit. Don't worry (he pronounced worry as *wary*), I'll still give you the ten cent tour." He laughed. "You'll love it, baby. Might not even wanna go back to B-More."

"I don't know about all that," Terrell said, concealing the notion that he would leap to become a permanent resident if he thought it could save his ass.

Malik smiled. "You don't know about oll 'at 'cawse I haven't showed you around yet," he said. "There's my home sweet home."

Large and semi-detached, Malik's house stood at the end of a picturesque block that contrasted the unassuming landscape they'd just passed. The fencing outside of the home made Terrell think of a medieval courtyard. Two huge bay windows lined with beautiful plants and candles overlooked the front porch.

"Welcome to the Taj Mahal of Brooklyn," Malik said, a huge grin on his face. "Moms stays hookin' this house up." He opened a storm door that matched the fencing before turning his key in the inside door. "Wait 'til you see inside."

Terrell drank in the gleaming hardwood floors, fancy ceiling fans, and tasteful furniture, discarding his gloom for his friend's benefit. Malik had every reason to feel proud of the home he grew up in.

"Yo, this house needs to be in Better Homes and Gardens," Terrell said. He supposed that he would have felt genuine excitement about the place if he had come under different circumstances. For now, good acting would have to do.

Malik nodded. "Yeah. Mom's be doin' it up."

Terrell followed Malik as he descended into an expansive basement. "The laundry room's through there," Malik said, pointing. "The rest of the basement is mine." He plopped down on his bed. "You got a change of clothes in your bag-right?"

Terrell nodded.

"Well, you can g'head and get showered in the upstairs bathroom," Malik said. "You don't have to wary about anybody coming in. Moms won't be home 'til a little later and my stepfather's away on business."

Terrell let the warm shower water continue to wash over him long after he was clean, all the while thinking of bullshit answers to the questions Malik was sure to have. He felt surprised when his erstwhile roommate asked none, offering encouragement instead.

"Don't even wary about no girl problems, Baltimore," he said. "Just let me show you how to have fun, NYC style. If it's meant to be, you and shorty will get back up. Damn, you look tired. You wanna catch a nap or somethin'?"

Terrell nodded.

"I-ight, then. You can crash on my bunk, while I get the festivities prepared for tonight. But your ass is sleepin' on that cot, later." Malik pointed to the left of the bed. "You're good now, son. Don't wary 'bout nothin'." He pumped his fist. "My man Terrell, in NYC. I'm lovin' this, baby. It's a Friday, too! Sleep well 'cawse we goin' out tonight. You in NYC now, son. You might sleep, but the Rotten Apple don't!"

Terrell faked an excited smile. What he really felt was relief, knowing that he didn't have to look over his shoulder as long as he was in New York. He wished that he could stay until his problems blew over, but he knew that wouldn't happen. He knew that Brock would not sit and wait by while he regrouped in his safe haven. His cousin had to be dealt with, but he had no idea of how to do so.

II

Detective Tom Brunanski stewed in silence at his desk, lamenting catching the primary for the previous night's murder at Parkview Gardens. Although it had been less than 24 hours, he already doubted the likelihood of getting a clearance.

Brunanski had been a Baltimore City Cop for seventeen years, a Homicide cop for the last eleven. The violent nature of the "great" city of Baltimore had resulted in him working scores of cases in that time. He'd seen more than enough to predict when getting a clearance was untenable, so he knew right away that the murder of Charles Johnson was such a case.

The shooting victim had been a model citizen according to everyone Brunanski had questioned about him. He had worked hard, paid his bills on time, minded his own business and been good to his wife.

Brunanski had interviewed the slain man's wife earlier that day. Hell, he'd spent most of the day interviewing close family, neighbors, and co-workers. The consensus was that Johnson had no enemies and no vices beyond a beer or two at the end of a hard day's work and the love of a choice steak. So why had his murder been so well planned and executed?

The towels were the thing. The killer had used one or more of the cheap cotton kind you'd get from Wal-Mart or K-Mart. The killer hadn't anticipated CSU recovering fibers from the scene. The towel or towels had been placed over the barrel of the gun as makeshift silencers. That was why none of the neighbors had heard any gunshots. The whole thing smacked of the Godfather II. It was the sort of thing only a hit man or very thoughtful enemy would do.

The victim's wallet had been taken, but this was no robbery. A drugged out or nervous robber might get an itchy trigger finger, but he wouldn't use a jury-rigged silencer.

If it was the work of some gang member, a calling card would have been left. Today's gangs wanted to make the news for their vile deeds- the result of growing up as criminals in the Information Age. No publicity was bad publicity concerning the corrupting of impressionable youths. Besides, there was no known gang involvement in Parkview Gardens.

The authorities had the towel fibers, but they did not have the towels themselves, meaning they had no prints to go along with the lack of a single witness. Brunanski felt certain that this was not a case of people pretending not to see anything because they were afraid of the criminal element in the neighborhood. The people who lived in Parkview Gardens were working class folks, retirees, and college students. They were willing to assist the police in any effort to keep the criminal element from establishing any type of stronghold in their neighborhood.

Mr. Johnson had come home late, returning from a second job. The guy had been working that second job to save up to buy a house, for Christ's sake. The shooter had known this just as they had known that there wouldn't be anyone outside on at the time of the shooting. They had been certain that only a loud noise would bring people's attention. The Vito Andolini silencers had eliminated that concern.

The killer had taken the time to learn Mr. Johnson's comings and goings, as well as the pattern of activity in the apartment complex. Why would someone go through so much trouble to murder such an unassuming man?

Until Detective Brunanski could answer that question, the .38 slugs that had been recovered from the murder scene weren't worth the contents of used toilet tissue. He examined a copy of the ledger of residents who lived in the slain man's building, obtained from the Parkview Garden's rental office. He had only two residents left to interview: Phillip Hines and Terrell Hawkins.

III

Terrell swayed to the percussive sounds of the hip-hop group on stage, trying to forget about his troubles for a little while. Malik had awakened him for the outing a little after 9, introducing Terrell to his mother before they embarked for the club they were now in.

Mrs. Davis was a stout woman with a road map of curves. At least at first glance, none of those curves bulged. She had deep chocolate skin and lively brown eyes, hot pressed hair, and long patterned fingernails. Mrs. Davis had a pleasant, almost down home manner. Once she left earshot, Terrell joked that she must have been hot shit when she was younger.

"She still is hot shit to my stepfather," Malik said. "Plus, she makes cake workin' at the Trade Center." He nudged Terrell, throwing his voice to sound like an old buck slave. "Now don't let me catch you lookin' at my mama funny."

Malik's easy rapport with his mother made Terrell think of Mrs. Hawkins. He felt glad that he had asked Monet to tell her that he had gone to New York for a few days. Mrs. Hawkins might have thought it strange that Terrell didn't call her himself, but he feared that hearing her voice might make him want to confess everything that he was involved in. His guilt tormented him that much.

Although it seemed about twice as large, the club he and Malik were in reminded Terrell of the Sonar Lounge back in Baltimore. Like Sonar, the place appeared to have been a warehouse in its' previous incarnation. Like Sonar, the stage, bar, and huge dance floor all stood on one level, as did the far less than pristine restrooms.

Terrell observed the sea of swaying bodies, realizing that the revelers were more diverse than he was used to seeing in clubs back home. He saw blacks, whites, Hispanics, and Asians- all moving to the intoxicating sounds of pure hip hop. Backed by a live band, a quartet of energetic performers recited lyrics about partying and avoiding the pitfalls of life. Through three songs, Terrell did not hear any lyrics glorifying crime or degrading women. He snickered, thinking that the performers would never be famous.

Whether they achieved fame and wealth or not, the group (called Wolfpack) put on one hell of a show. Terrell's enjoyment of them increased as he consumed the two rum and cokes Malik brought him. Malik had reached legal drinking age in April, which rendered any concerns Terrell had about being carded moot. His host was more than happy to go back and forth to the bar.

"This is a real hip-hop spot," Malik said, ceasing dancing with a pretty Asian girl long enough to utter in Terrell's ear. "You like this shit-don't you?"

"Hell yeah!" Terrell grinned, free arm swaying to the music while the other held his latest drink.

Malik laughed. "I knew you'd be feelin' this spot," he said, shuffling back over to the Asian beauty.

They partied into the wee hours of the night before catching a cab home. Feeling a nice buzz, Terrell was glad that Malik elected not to ride the subway. Within minutes of entering Malik's house, Terrell fell into a peaceful sleep, enjoying a temporary respite from the nightmarish concerns that plagued him.

IV

Detectives Martin Dunbar and Charles Douglass sat at their combined wits' end, drinking harsh black coffee in a greasy spoon on the Avenue in Hampden. Their breakfast sandwiches sat undisturbed. Their booth sat farthest from the glass front door – cops' seats for cops. The proprietor of the Northwest Baltimore haunt was used to officers coming in, even out of district ones like Douglass and Dunbar, whom hailed from the Northeast Precinct.

Once a few cops took a liking to an eatery or bar, word traveled fast and it soon became a cop hangout. Such was the case with this neighborhood diner. It served as an ideal pit stop for a hungry civil servant, opening at six a.m., seven days a week and serving good but cheap breakfast and coffee. The cops that stopped in almost always choose to sit at one of the diner's eight booths, only sitting at the counter if none were available.

During their three years as partners, Detectives Dunbar and Douglass had developed a number of preferred practices that they used while working a case together. Meeting to brainstorm ideas on a Saturday morning was not one of them. They both believed that weekends were for the wife and kids, having seen the personal lives of far too many detectives fall into shambles during the obsessive pursuit of cases.

Dunbar was Douglass's senior by fourteen chronological years and by ten years on the force. He had been married for eighteen years and fathered three strapping boys. The oldest was 16, followed by a 12-year old and a 9-year old. Douglass and his lovely wife had celebrated their third anniversary a few weeks back. Their adorable daughter Morganna was two years old. Unlike many of their colleagues who viewed family and personal relationships as something to squeeze in around the job, these two men refused to treat their loved one as afterthoughts. This shared reverence of family was one of the things that made the detectives' partnership so effective. Only the most extraordinary of circumstances could pull these men away from their homes on a Saturday. The pursuit of the Lake Montebello killer/killers qualified as such.

Other than the ease with which they concluded how and why the victims were killed, they hadn't made any progress after nearly two weeks of long hours working the case.

A battery of interviews left all three victims painted as serious party girls. Douglass and Dunbar believed that their wild reputations were deserved, concluding that the victims had hooked up with some guys in pursuit of a good time. All parties involved had gotten drunk or high or both in the lead up to some sucking and fucking.

Due to the loss of trace evidence that resulted from weeks of underwater decay, the medical examiner hadn't been able to confirm sexual activity, but there had been enough left of the victims to determine the causes of their deaths. Based on the ME's findings, the detectives concluded that at some point during the party/orgy, horseplay got out of hand and Tia Jenkins suffered a fatal blow to the head. After that, the other two girls had been smothered so that they couldn't tell. As gruesome as it was, the dismemberment of the bodies served occurred only as an effort to conceal the murders.

Chopping the victims up and disposing of them in Lake Montebello had been a stroke of criminal genius. It could be argued that divine providence was responsible for one of the girl's heads coming free of its' mooring and drifting to the shore. Douglass joked that the doers must have shit a brick when the story hit the news.

Yes, figuring out how and why the girls were killed had been easy. Coming up with a strong suspect had so far proved to be impossible.

The problem was that the girls had all been so damn slutty. To describe them as promiscuous would be like saying the Grand Canyon was a big hole. In a week's time, Douglass, Dunbar and some other detectives whom had been assigned to back them up had interviewed more than thirty people. Twenty one of the interviewees had been young men whom had been acquainted with the victims. Every one of those acquaintances claimed that they had not seen the girls on the night in question, although quite a few of them admitted to having had a good time with them before. There was talk of things the sisters had done - things that might send a church lady into cardiac arrest.

There was not as much talk of Heloise Hopkins' exploits, but the detectives believed in the birds of a feather axiom. Maybe Heloise had just been growing into her whorishness, or maybe she was just a good deal more discreet than her friends.

Working the Lake Montebello case had taken a toll to Detective Douglass. He found himself worrying about what kind of young woman his adorable toddler would grow up to be. If he had any say in the matter, she wasn't going to be a street running wild thing who gave it away like it was going out of style.

The detectives agreed that no matter what kind of lives the victims had led, they didn't deserve to be murdered, chopped up and thrown into a lake. Their grieving families deserved to see their killers caught and punished. Douglass and Dunbar pondered how they would be affected if their families were confronted with such a loss. They felt more driven to solve this case than any in recent memory.

The detectives' professional reasons for wanting to solve this case were just as paramount as their personal ones. The killings were an anomaly in Baltimore- a triple murder that wasn't drug related. It had been big news in the area- the type of high profile case known as a red ball in Baltimore Police Department parlance. Though they enjoyed detective work, both Douglass and Dunbar desired career advancement and putting a case like this in the black would be the equivalent of finding a golden ticket. The rub was that doing so seemed less likely with each passing day.

None of the young men the detectives had interviewed seemed any guiltier than the next. The well practiced partners had tried to intimidate and confuse many of them, but none of them had lost their cool. Phone records indicated that at last eight of the so called suspects had spoken with at least one of the victims on the last night they were seen, but when questioned about it they all explained that they had talked to the girls to string them along, so that they could line up another good time. That recurring explanation rang true to the detectives. They'd both had their share of the slutty type in their salad days – so they knew how it was.

The detectives figured that sluts of the new millennium weren't so different from sluts of the previous one. Such types were still willing to do any slutty thing as long as you pretended to give a fuck about them. Part of that deal was calling and bullshitting with them sometime other than when you wanted to fuck or get blown.

The detectives decided to try a different approach after springing the fact of their phone records on a mustachioed kid named Alonzo and getting another calm explanation. They reasoned that it had taken several guys to kill the girls and dispose of their bodies. They learned the acquaintances of those whom had communicated with the victims by phone and tried to play them against each other. It was a tactic they had used on Shawntae Kennard and Terrell Hawkins after discovering that Damon Brock had spoken to the Jenkins girls. That approach had proven no more effective than the straightforward track.

"We're staring at a brick wall, Marty," Douglass said. "All we got is a bunch of guys who were either fucking the victims or lining themselves up to fuck the victims."

"Yeah," Dunbar agreed, pushing the plate that bore his BLT aside. "The problem is any of the guys we questioned could have done it. None of them acted particularly guilty. If we had some way of narrowing it down, we could put the squeeze on somebody-maybe see if we could trip them up. But none of those guys stood out from the others. We could roust the same guys again, but it's hard to scare a suspect when they know you got no evidence." He sighed. "I don't know about this one, partner."

Douglass sipped his coffee. "You think we might not clear the case?"

Dunbar shook his head. "We might not clear any case we get. What I'm thinking is that we probably won't clear this case. A huge fucking red ball and it seems like we don't have a snowball's chance in hell of clearing it. Don't give me that look, Douglass. Unless we get some type of freak break, we're stuck on this one."

"Fuck!" Douglass banged on the table, causing their coffee mugs to rattle and drawing curious glances from the other breakfast patrons. "You're probably right. This shit pisses me off."

"You know something, partner?" Dunbar pushed his plate farther away. "I'm not so hungry just now. Let's finish this coffee and get out of here."

They were about to do just that when Detective Thomas Brunanski strolled through the greasy spoon's front door.

V

“What brings you out so early on a Saturday morning?” Dunbar asked, smirking as Brunanski slid his tall, burly frame in next to Douglass. “I’ve always known you to keep a vampire’s hours.”

“And I’ve never known you family men to talk shop on the weekend,” Brunanski rejoined. A waitress with wide shoulders and boulders for a bust line approached him.

“What kin I do you for, Hon?” her scratchy voice confessed years of chain smoking.

Dunbar resumed shop talk after the waitress left to fill Brunanski’s order of bacon, egg, and cheese on white toast and the blackest coffee possible.

“You know we’re the primaries in the Lake Montebello Case?”

Brunanski shrugged. “Who in Batimore PD doesn’t know you guys are working that huge fucking red ball? You guys got enough help with that or what?”

“We got enough help, alright. All help means in this case is half a dozen frustrated detectives instead of just two. We got no real leads, no DNA, no murder weapon. This case is as cold as Antarctica right now.”

“We decided to meet up here and brainstorm- come up with some fresh ideas on how to tackle it,” Douglass said.

“You guys come up with anything?”

"Fuck no." Dunbar frowned. "Good police work can only carry us so far on this one. We need a break in the worst way. This fucking case is a stone whodunit."

Douglass nodded. "Boulder size."

Dunbar laughed without humor. "Fucking Rocky Mountains size."

The waitress returned. "Here's your coffee, Hon."

Brunanski inspected the contents of the mug for proper blackness before thanking her.

She nodded. "Your sandwich'll be right out."

Douglass watched Brunanski as Brunanski watched the waitress depart. "You like a big boned woman like that, Hon?" he pitched his voice into an almost spot on impersonation of the server.

Brunanski chuckled. "I like anything with tits and a pulse to start with. The problem is what to do with them after you've exchanged fluids a few times. Anyway, don't expect me to cry about you guys' red ball. I just pulled a shit case, myself. Thursday night some working stiff gets popped over at Parkview Gardens apartments. Shooter tried to make it look like a robbery, but this was no robbery. The doer came out of nowhere, pops the guy using a hand towel around the gun barrel as a silencer."

"Just like the Godfather II," the partners spoke and nodded in unison.

"Yup. Then the guy wraps the towel around the barrel again- either that or uses a second towel- and pops the poor schmo in the head while he's lying on the ground. My first instinct was that the thing looked like a hit, but the doer made mistakes that indicate otherwise."

The waitress appeared with Brunanski's sandwich. He exchanged the customary pleasantries of server and customer before returning to his riveted audience.

"The first thing is he left fabric from the towel or towels on the ground. The second thing- and this is a big one- is he didn't pick up the spent shells. What kind of hit man has the smarts to kill a guy using makeshift silencers - stalks the guy well enough to know when to get him without anyone else being out and about- does all that and leaves shells around? It's like the doer was professional and inept at the same time. Besides wouldn't a real hit man have a real silencer- not some jury rigged shit?"

Dunbar shrugged. "Maybe the hitman was low budget."

Brunanski dismissed the notion with a wave of his hand. "And who the fuck would want to hit this poor guy anyway? I mean this guy was a solid citizen, average Joe to the max. The guy had no known enemies, wasn't in to anyone for money. He was Mr. Respectable- a well liked working stiff."

"And now he's just a stiff stiff." Dunbar couldn't resist a morbid attempt at humor.

Brunanski begrudged a smile before sipping his coffee. "Come up with some fresh material, Marty," he said. "Anyway, that's what's got me up so early. Truth be told, I barely went to bed."

"You got any leads?" Douglass asked.

Brunanski took another sip. "Not yet. I got two of the vic's neighbors left to interview. One supposedly spent the night with a girlfriend. The other is some college kid. His mom told me he just went out of town."

A light bulb flicked on in Douglass's mind. "College kid? You say the murder happened in Parkview Gardens apartments?"

"Yeah." Brunanski's brows leapt at the younger detective's sudden excitement. "Whaddaya think you know something?"

"Could be." Douglass's fingers strummed the tabletop. "You got the name of the college kid- the one who left town?" Dunbar watched his partner in silent curiosity, wondering what the younger man thought he was putting together.

Brunanski pulled a tiny note pad from his back pocket and read from the top page. "Terrell Hawkins."

Douglass rapped on the table, his smile revealing new hope. "That's the kid from the P.A.L. Center, Marty."

Dunbar smiled just as big as his partner. "Well, I'll be damned."

"What's with you guys?" Brunanski asked.

"The esteemed Thomas Brunanski." Dunbar stood and walked to the other side of the booth, clapping Brunanski on a beefy shoulder. "Detective- you may have just given us the break we need."

VI

All three men consumed their food with enthusiasm as Douglass and Dunbar connected the dots for their potential savior.

It was all too big a coincidence to be unconnected. One of the potential suspects of the biggest non drug-related crime in the city in years has an upstairs neighbor murdered not long after being questioned by the police? A neighbor who despite having no known enemies or illicit vices was basically assassinated? Who would kill a man with no known enemies in such an efficient and witness free fashion?

Douglass and Dunbar felt certain that it had to be someone who thought the victim knew too much. Although his leaving town right after Mr. Johnson's murder smacked of guilt, neither of the detectives suspected Terrell as the doer. They couldn't see a college kid working for pennies at a P.A.L. Center doing something as cold-blooded as that, not when they knew of someone whom seemed far more likely.

The cool smugness of Terrell's cousin Damon Brock rushed to mind. Knowing what Brunanski had revealed about Mr. Johnson's murder made it seem plausible that young Mr. Brock was up to his neck in this mess. Reflecting on their encounter with him spurred the conclusion that he was just smart enough to try to pull off something like Mr. Johnson's murder and just dumb enough to leave the slugs at the scene.

Their plates clean, each of the detectives worked on a second cup of coffee as Douglass recounted their initial encounter with the little wise ass.

They came upon him sauntering down the marble stoop of his grandmother's East Baltimore row house. Short, slight, and ebony skinned, he rubbed sleep from his eyes. His car keys jangled as he approached the driver's side door of a huge chocolate brown Cutlass Supreme. Having something of a sweet tooth for large American cars, Douglass pegged the gleaming vehicle as a 1986 model.

He and his partner stepped out of their vehicle and approached the young man. "Are you Damon Brock?" Douglass asked.

"Yes, I am.... Cop," Brock said, making the last word sound like profanity. "Whatchall want wit me? I'm on my own way to work."

He pointed to the lettering on his Department of Parks and Recreation work shirt. "See, I'm a civil servant just like y'all."

"You might be a civil servant," Dunbar said, warming up for his usual bad cop performance. "But you're nothing like us."

Brock sized Dunbar up. "You right. I'm half the man you are ... Big Guy. Guess that's just proof that Jesus loves me."

"If you're worried about getting to work on time, you won't prolong this encounter with wisecracks," Douglass said.

Brock raised his arms in mock surrender. "Aight, man. Aight. I'll try not to give y'all a hard time. It's just that cops ain't that well liked in this neighborhood."

He looked toward the huge blue light and camera mounted atop a street pole that overlooked a liquor store at the end of the block. Around the clock surveillance in down-trodden neighborhoods was a measure enacted two years earlier by a mayor desperate to reduce the depressing level of violent crime in the city he presided over. The move had engendered a lot of resentment in neighborhoods where the cameras were present. Talk of civil rights being violated became a common theme. Many cops felt that only people who were up to no good should be bothered by them.

"Yeah?" Dunbar retorted. "Well the criminals in this neighborhood ain't well liked by cops."

Brock shrugged. “I don’t know nothin’ about no criminals. Kin y’all git to the point?”

“Sure.” Douglass gave Dunbar a look that said 'Let me handle this'. “We’d just like to know where you were on the night of June 10th.”

“Man, that was a couple weeks ago. What the hell y’all need to know that for?”

“You heard about the three girls that were found chopped up in Lake Montebello?”

“Who hasn’t? I do watch the news. Just cuz I live in East Baltimore don’t make me totally ignorant.”

Ignoring Brock’s last remark, Douglass said, “But did you know the victims personally? Before you answer that last question, I should inform you that we have cell phone records showing that you talked to one of the victims on June 10th- the last night they were seen alive.”

In the split second after Douglass’s revelation, a war of emotions played out on Brock’s face. The beginning of a panicked expression lost out to a too cool for school grin. The detectives didn’t have to glance at each other to communicate the shared notion that if Brock did have anything to do with the murders, he wouldn’t be easy to crack.

“I wouldn’t say night,” Brock said, the grin now painted on his face. “It was still light out when I called that chick.”

“So you did speak with her that evening?”

The grin shifted into a scowl. “What the hell kind of game you cops playin’? You jus’ told me you had phone records of me speakin’ wit’ the whore- so why you askin' me shit you already know? I told y'all I gotta git to work."

"Whore? You don't have a lot of respect for the dead- do you?"

"It ain't disrespectful to call 'em like I see 'em. I didn't know the one chick, but them sistas was straight up gutta ball sluts. Real microwaves- feel me? Muthafuckin' meat lockas. They were known for doin' all kinds a nasty shit. Tha's why me 'n' my boys wanted to hook up wit 'em."

"So, I take it that the hook up didn't happen?"

Brock smirked. "Naw, man. You had to git in line early wit' them. Tell you one thing, though- If they woulda hooked up wit' us, they'd be alright right now. Niggas woulda just passed them bitches around, then sent 'em home when we were done."

Douglass frowned. "You speak of them as if they were objects."

Brock laughed. "Git the fuck outta here! Are you a cop or a fuckin' church pasta, man? Shit, them bitches acted like objects, so they got treated like they got treated. Don't try to act like cops don't be bangin' slut ass bitches, too. I know how y'all do."

He smirked as he looked at Douglass's wedding band. "I bet you got a lil freak stashed somewhere. 'Specially the way some bitches get moist for detectives. You got that fake Michael Jordan look, too…you problee don't even have to pay for it like Frosty the Fatman, here."

Detective Dunbar flushed red and clenched his jaw, managing not to rise to the bait.

Brock chuckled and glanced at his watch. "Kin we wrap this shit up?"

"Sure," Douglass said. "All you have to do is tell us where you were that night."

"Fuck, man," Brock grumbled, leaning against the car. "Lemme think about it for a second. That shit was a long fuckin' time ago."

One elbow rested on the car. Brock closed his opposite hand and raised it to his chin, selling how hard he was thinking about his answer. Douglass moved his hands up and down, urging his partner to keep cool, knowing that Dunbar was fighting the urge to manhandle the little shit.

"Oh, yeah," Brock said, straightening up. "That was the night of that big storm. Me 'n' my boys tried to connect wit' some other bitches after Tia 'n' 'em fronted on us. We ain't have no luck, though. Freaks make up their mind about how they gon' git fucked early on Fridays. So, we ended up goin' to the movies out White Marsh." He laughed. "We was in that bitch drinkin', pourin' Bacardi in our soda cups. I was a little nice by the time the movie let out, feel me? Thing is, we got stuck in the theater cuz a storm was goin' full blast by then. We had to wait in the lobby a long time before it calmed down enough for us to even see our way to the car. Even after it calmed down some, we still got soak 'n' wet."

Douglass nodded. "I remember that storm now. I hadn't connected the two events in my mind before you mentioned it. What do you think about that, partner?"

Dunbar smirked. "I think that a storm like that would provide perfect cover for anyone looking to dump a body or two- or three. Hell, there wouldn't be any other sane people out and about during nasty weather like that. I know I made sure my big white ass was under shelter that night."

Another split second war of emotions played out on Brock's face. An expression of concern that he might've said too much struggled to assert itself, only to be beaten back by another that read that he could care less about this entire exchange. Brock threw in a shoulder shrug as a side order.

"We digress," Douglass said. "What time do you think you left the theater?"

Brock scratched his head. "It was problee like 1:00 in the mornin'. Like I said, we had to wait in the lobby a long time before we jus' said 'fuck it' and ran to the car."

"What movie did you see?" Douglass spat the question out, hoping to catch Brock by surprise.

Brock wasn't the least bit flustered. "What the hell does that matter?"

"Just answer the question."

"Spider Man. That was a good fuckin' movie! I ain't think it would be good like the comic book, but I was wrong. The only thang is that broad in the movie wasn't thick like Mary Jane is in the comics. She was still fine, though. I'd fuck her skinny white a-"

"We're not interested in your movie critiques," Douglass cut him off. "What time did the movie start?"

"Damn, man. You expectin' me to rememba a lot about a night when I couldn't git no pussy. Iss not like that shit was a special occasion for me." He shrugged. “I think it was like 10:00, maybe 10:30. The movie was long as shit.”

Douglass nodded. “One last thing.”

Brock cocked an eyebrow.

“Who are these boys you speak of?”

Brock started to answer, then shook his head. “Nope. I’m not tellin’ y’all that.”

“Without anyone to confirm it, your alibi isn’t worth anything.”

“Oh, I’m sure ya’ll find out who they are. It ain’t no big secret. I’m jus’ not tellin’ you. I don’t have to make your job easier, ‘specially since none of us are involved in the shit you talkin’ ‘bout. I don’t see nothin’ wrong in inconveniencin’ y’all like y’all are inconveniencin’ me. You’re stupid if you think I’m gon’ make it easier for y’all to fuck wit’ my friends. Y’all are detectives. Go detect that shit.”

He added a final flourish to the hard time he was giving them, holding his wrists out as if waiting to be handcuffed. “Now unless you have reason to arrest me, I’d like to go the fuck to work.”

VII

“I wanted to kick his fucking ass right then,” a smirking Dunbar punctuated his partner’s story. “But we didn’t see any reason to suspect him more than any of the victims’ other admirers. His buddies backed up his story even though we tried to trip them up. And the girls did talk to other guys after their call with him.”

"We thought he was a real asshole," Douglass said. "But so were half of the other knuckleheads we interviewed. Those girls definitely didn't go in for the well-mannered type." He slapped the table before eyeing Brunanski with reverence. "But now we're back in the hunt. Thanks to Ole Mr. Solo Flight."

"If I didn't know you better, I'd think that look on your face means you wanna blow me," Brunanski deadpanned, causing them all to burst into laughter.

"Nah. I'd sooner hump an antelope than go gay. But the thought of solving this case does make my dick hard."

The detectives ordered another round of coffee. They sipped the hot brew at a leisurely pace while Douglass and Dunbar discussed how to turn the heat up on Damon Brock. Based on their first interviews with them, the partners didn't think that Terrell or Shawntae were capable of doing what had been done to those girls. On the other hand, someone who disdained women as much as Brock seemed very capable of doing that kind of damage given the right set of circumstances. Also, Brock was the only one of the three to have a police record, having been arrested once for assault and another time for drunk and disorderly conduct. That wasn't much of a jacket compared to a lot of young guys in Baltimore, but everyone crawls before they walk.

The first girl, Tia - the one who died of the head trauma - was probably an accident. After that, a switch flipped in Brock. He decided that getting rid of the other two girls was a far better alternative than being thrown at the mercy of the law. His "boys" just didn't have the faculties to take control of such a horrible situation.

Did they help him kill the other girls? It was a possibility, but Detective Douglass argued that most likely they had stood by, feeling powerless to stop him. Detective Dunbar agreed that he had not seen the hardness of a practiced criminal in either Terrell or Shawntae. The detectives concluded that although they probably hadn't helped kill the girls, Terrell and Shawntae had to have helped dispose of the bodies. A small guy like Brock couldn't have dismembered the bodies and dispatched them into the lake without help. If all of those assumptions were correct, then offering Terrell and Shawntae a deal might be enough to turn one or both of them.

The detectives surmised that Brock and Co. had brought the girls back to Terrell's apartment that night. At some point when they were partying, Mr. Johnson went downstairs and asked them to keep the noise down.

Sometime after the case became a red ball, Brock decided that Mr. Johnson had seen one or all of the girls when he came to the door. That's when he decided to kill the poor guy. The detectives figured that Brock had taken care of Mr. Johnson without consulting the others. Terrell had panicked after he found out, heading to New York to get out of the hot zone.

If the detectives' assumptions were correct, then Terrell had to be terrified of his cousin by now. That meant that Terrell was the strongest candidate for folding under pressure.

The detectives all agreed that Brunanski didn't need to bother with questioning Phillip Hines. Instead, he would seek out Shawntae Kennard and see how he responded to a new wave of pressure. Douglass and Dunbar would share the pleasure of paying another visit to Mr. Brock. As for the matter of Terrell Hawkins's trip to New York, there were ways of influencing him to hasten his return.

# Chapter Eight

I

Marian Taylor felt sick with worry, having heard nothing from her son since Thursday evening. Before Shawntae left, he told her that he was going to spend the night at Darlene's place.

Hearing those words had done Marian's heart wonders. Though her sole offspring and the mother of her grandchild had been on and off for some time, she hoped that the young parents would settle down with each other someday. She didn't want Tae to be in and out of his son's life the way Tae's father had been in and out of his.

That concern paled in comparison to the fear that now gripped Ms. Taylor. She'd spoken with Darlene on Friday. The young woman told her that Shawntae had rushed into the night after a phone call, refusing to say where he was going. No one had heard from him since.

Ms. Taylor had called his job to see if he was there, but he wasn't scheduled for work again until Sunday afternoon. She had dialed her son's good friend Brock, only to learn that he hadn't seen Shawntae in a couple of days. "Knowin' him," Brock said, "He's problee caught up wit' some new girl 'n' lost track of time. He'll turn up just fine Ms. Taylor. You'll see."

Ms. Taylor hoped that Brock was right, but she took no comfort in his sentiments. Shawntae had always been good about notifying her when he expected to be off somewhere. She tried Tae's friend Terrell several times, but got no answer.

Now she sat alone in her parlor. Her shaky hand struggled to grasp the glass of heavily sweetened lemonade that she drank from. Doctor Gambril would admonish her if he could see her now, saying that she knew better than to consume something so sugar laden. Well, if he was here now, she'd look him right in the eye and tell him to leave her be. Even a Christian woman had to partake of something to calm her nerves and a sugary drink was a sight better than alcohol or Prozac, insulin level be damned. She felt certain that managing his glucose level would be the last thing on Doctor Gambril's mind if he stepped into her shoes.

The buzzing of her front doorbell interrupted Ms. Taylor's racing thoughts. She sat her glass aside, passing through her immaculate kitchen and living room to answer it. Someone who stuck out like a sore thumb in her neighborhood stood on the other side of her peephole. The only white guys who passed through her block in sharp suits were salesmen or detectives, and the man bore no wares. Ms. Taylor placed a hand over her fluttering heart, hoping that the big cop had not come to serve notice of her son's death.

"Please, Lord. Please." Her lips trembled as she clasped her hands and looked skyward. "Anything but that."

The lawman buzzed the doorbell again.

"Please, Lord," she pleaded once more before placing her hand on the doorknob.

The man turned to face the street, perhaps about to walk away. He whirled back around when the door creaked open.

"May I help you?" Ms. Taylor spoke through the screen door.

The beefy cop wore an impassive expression on his face. "Yes. Ma'am, I'm detective Thomas Brunanski of the Baltimore City Police Department."

He held out his badge. She glanced at it and nodded, unable to make out the inscription without her reading glasses. "What kind of detective are you?" she asked, dreading the answer.

"I'm with the Homicide Division."

Ms. Taylor felt a tremor in her chest.

"I'm looking for Shawntae Kennard," the detective continued in his affect less tone. "I need to ask him some questions pertaining to a case that I'm investigating."

Ms. Taylor stood silent, trying to process what the policeman had just said.

"Ma'am, is Shawntae here?"

"No my son isn't here!" she exploded. "He's been missing since Thursday night! I filed a missing persons report late last night! Now you come here saying you have questions for him? Well, he can't very well answer your questions when no one knows where he is. Can he?"

A shower of tears escaped Ms. Taylor's eyes. She hated crying in front of this- this cop. But she just couldn't help herself.

"I apologize, Ma'am." An undertone of guilt crept into Detective Brunanski's voice. "I had no idea that your son was missing."

Ms. Taylor continued to lash out. "Don't you policeman talk to each other? You should have gotten your facts straight before you came bothering me. When I saw you out there, I thought you had come to tell me Shawntae was dead- just like the detectives serve notice to families on those cop shows. Now, I'm more upset than I was before!"

She wiped her tears with the back of her right hand, then started to close the inside door. A shout from the detective halted hear. "Just a minute, Ma'am!"

Ms. Taylor poked her head around the half closed door.

Detective Brunanski's voice shrunk into a near whisper when he spoke next. "One more thing, please."

Ms. Taylor treated him to the harshest scowl she could muster. "What is it?"

Brunanski sighed. "You say your son was last seen Thursday night. Would you happen to know the time?"

"All I can tell you is that it was late. If you want to know exactly when, you'll have to ask my grandson's mother."

II

Shawntae's girlfriend told Detective Brunanski that he had left her residence well after 11 p.m. on the night in question. Upon examining the body, the ME had concluded that Mr. Johnson was murdered at least an hour prior to that.

The disconsolate young woman said that Shawntae had rushed out after a phone call, saying that he was going to walk down to the nearest intersection to flag down a cab or a hack. He'd refused to say where he was going or who his phone call had been with. She cried as she told the detective how she regretted having lost her temper, calling Shawntae every cuss word in the book and trying to pry his cell phone from him in front of their young son. He had shaken her off, promising to explain everything when he came back.

She'd cursed him all the way to the door, telling him not to bother coming back, saying that she'd had it with his bullshit.

Darlene confided to Detective Brunanski that she had thought Shawntae was going to see another girl. She prayed that the angry words she'd said were not the last ones she would ever speak to the father of her child.

Brunanski only added fuel to the inferno that had been lit under Detectives Douglass and Dunbar when he shared those revelations. The partners envisioned a scenario in which Terrell and Shawntae confronted Brock after learning of Mr. Johnson's death. That confrontation had resulted in Shawntae being M.I.A. and Terrell fleeing to New York. If the detectives' speculations were correct, they just might be able to break the case. Brunanski would pay a visit to Terrell's mother, making her believe that they suspected him of having a significant role in everything that had transpired, including his friend's disappearance.

They figured that she'd contact her son as soon as Brunanski left. Not wanting to have to take the weight for the murders, Terrell would hurry back to Baltimore. He'd be ready to talk then.

Douglass and Dunbar salivated at the prospect of paying Damon Brock another visit. Informing him of how close he was to being cornered would be a delicious privilege. They couldn't wait to see fear replace the familiar smug expression on his face.

III

Douglass and Dunbar spotted their quarry leaving the Papa John's Pizza on 33rd and Barclay. "Moonlighting, are we?" Dunbar said, grinning at him. The detective stood in front of the driver's side door of his own late model Buick sedan.

"What the hell, man?" Brock hissed, pointing to his green unifom shirt. "I just started this job part time 'n' y'all are here harrassin' me? This is my second night workin'. Y'all tryna git me fired already?"

"You got us all wrong," Dunbar said. "We'd hate to make you look bad in front of your new employers. But, we do need to talk to you. So how about we follow you during your little delivery- then you give us a few minutes of your time?"

"Did my granmova tell y'all where to find me?"

Dunbar shrugged. "I guess she thought it was better for us to find you here than for us to keep coming to her door."

Brock scowled. "Whateva, man. I got three deliveries- so iss gon' be a minute."

Dunbar grinned larger than before. "Fine by us. We've both canceled our Saturday night plans already."

After his last delivery, Brock pulled over at 33rd and Saint Paul- a busy thoroughfare a few blocks north of his place of work. "What- are y'all fishin' again?" he asked, miming a yawn as he got out of his car. He leaned against the driver's side door as if he didn't have a care in the world.

"You might say that," Douglass answered. "But this time we have better equipment."

Brock laughed. "It don't matta what kind of equipment you got if there's no fish where you cast the line."

"He's got a point, partner," Dunbar said. "So whaddaya think? Are we casting our line in the right stream?"

Douglass nodded. "The water looks bountiful from here."

Tired of the wordplay, Brock reverted to vulgarity. "Man-what the fuck do y'all want?"

Douglass smiled. "We just wanted to let you know how our investigation of those girls' murders is going."

"Like I should give a fuck."

"Oh, but you should," Dunbar said, looking set to bust his considerable gut. "See- like you said the first time we interviewed you - those girls were some real wild ones. They might have been with anyone that night. That's why we've been stuck in the investigation. There are at least eight different groups of friends they could have been with, including your little crew. Without witnesses to place anyone with them or sufficient physical evidence, we had no way of pinpointing exactly who the lucky bunch was. Douglass and I were pretty much at our wits' end."

"That was before a pair of remarkable coincidences," Douglass chimed in, eyes gleaming as bright as his partner's. "Seems one of your cousin Terrell's neighbors was murdered right outside of his apartment building Thursday night."

"So?" Brock shrugged.

"Funny that you should say 'so'," Dunbar said, his tone sarcastic. "Why not ask if it was someone you knew? After all, logic would dictate that you might know the guy. I think it's a safe assumption, what with you spending so much time over there."

Brock furrowed his brow. "Who told you I spend so much time ova there?" A tiny vein pulsed in his forehead. "My granmova? Cuz her old ass don't know shit about me. She only thinks she does."

Dunbar looked at Brock as if he had said something very stupid. "Why would she have to tell us that? It just seems logical, that's all. Naturally, if your cousin has a bachelor pad and you don't, you're going to spend a lot of time over there."

"It's not like you young fellas could get trashed and chase pussy at Grandma's house," Douglass added.

"Y'all are enjoyin' this so much," Brock grumbled.

Dunbar snickered. "Maybe we wouldn't like it so much if you didn't try to be such a hard ass," he said. "But how rude of me to interrupt. Please continue, partner. You're more eloquent with this sort of thing than I am."

"Thanks, partner." Douglass touched fists with the heavier man.

Brock appeared to be on the verge of passing steam from his ears and nose. His anger pleased Detective Douglass to no end. "As my partner so logically reasoned, it would be perfectly normal for the three of you to bring some girls over to Terrell's apartment. You all are having a good time. Maybe everybody's good and smashed. Rowdy young people that you are; you start making a lot of noise. This poor sap who got shot- Mr. Johnson - he lived directly upstairs from Terrell. He's married and ain't nearly as young as you guys-hell, maybe his wife nagged him into it. Whatever the case, he comes downstairs and asks if you wouldn't mind keeping it down. You all quickly agree and then go on about your business. Later on, one of the girls gets hurt, probably accidentally. Accidents happen. You know?"

Douglass watched Brock like a hawk as he spoke, wanting to see if the suspect betrayed any alarm. An outraged scowl greeted him instead. Douglass smiled at his quarry, thinking that Brock knew they were close now.

"It's an accident, but you guys panic. Nobody wants to go to jail and the other girls start making a scene. So you have to shut them up. You don't want to. You just have to. Then you get rid of them- hack them up and toss them into the lake. There was a terrible storm that night, so no one was out and about to see what you did. At first you're scared, but then day after day goes by and you feel like you're home free. But then some freak occurrence happens, or maybe an act of God. The next thing you know, Lake Montebello's been combed and all of the girls' remains have been found. The case is all over the local news and even gets some national attention- what we cops call a red ball. So you guys think of an alibi. We come around and question all of you, but you know we're just reaching. We got no real evidence and you guys are just one possibility among many. Still, just knowing what you've done hangs a cloud of fear over all of you. You start thinking about what happened all the time, about making sure that you get away with it."

He pointed at Brock. "Maybe you get a little obsessed with it. Finally you decide that the now deceased Mr. Johnson might be a loose string that needs tying. Maybe he saw one or all of the girls when he came to the door that night. Maybe it hasn't dawned on him yet, but one day he'll put it together. Maybe if he does, it destroys your alibi. Maybe you just couldn't take the chance."

"Maybe tha's a buncha bullshit," Brock growled. "Maybe you should quit bein' a detective 'n' start writin' detective stories. You could make a lotta money wit' that fucked up imagination."

"I wasn't finished."

"Oh, Jesus," Brock groaned, flailing his hands about. "Go on, man. Jus' make it quick. Saturday is a busy night for Papa John's."

"I'll give you the abridged version, then. We figure you killed Mr. Johnson on your own. You tried to make it look like a robbery, but you shot him too clean. Plus fabric from the towels you used as silencers were discovered at the scene. You got that from the Godfather II, right? Hell of a movie. Anyway, Stevie Wonder could see that what happened to Mr. Johnson was personal. But he had no known enemies. The detective who drew the case wasn't fooled and neither were your friends. They figured out that you had done it and confronted you about it. During that confrontation, things get out of hand. You pull the gun you used on poor Mr. Johnson just to scare them, but there's a struggle. Shawntae gets hurt or maybe dead and Terrell gets as far away from you as possible. Did you know Shawntae hasn't been seen since Thursday night?"

Douglass chuckled, not waiting for Brock to respond. "How stupid of me to ask? Of course you wouldn't admit to such a thing. You're much too smart to incriminate yourself. I think you really might not have known that

Terrell blew town, though. Nobody's sure where he went. Whatever happened between you guys must have put a real scare into him."

Dunbar couldn't resist joining in. "He's probably so scared that he'll cooperate with us as soon as we get to him. After that the only job you'll have is playing the waiting game. Waiting for the needle, that is."

"Or you could confess," Douglass said. "If you confess maybe the prosecutor will cut you a break. Life in prison instead of the needle."

"Y-y-you fuckin' cops are sick," Brock said, a stammer seizing brief hold of his speech. "Everything that you just said to me is bullshit! If Tae is missin', this is the first I heard of it. I haven't exactly had time to be checking for him, what wit' startin' a new job 'n' shit. As for Terrell's neighbor, iss a shame. Iss always a shame when people git killed in Baltimore, but they keep right on gittin' killed. Don't they? You say he had no known enemies, but niggas lead all kinds of secret lives now days. Maybe he had a gamblin' problem or a drug problem or somethin'. Not that I need to explain that, cuz I had no dealin's wit' the dude. As far as Terrell is concerned, I ain't know it was against the law for a nigga to leave town. Maybe he went to see his roommate up in New York. That ain't for me to worry about. I wasn't seein' him that much anyway. Let his girl trouble herself over that shit. She's the one he's always up unda."

"What's this girfriend's name?" Douglass asked.

Brock laughed. "Man figga that shit out for ya self. I feel sorry for you cops. You ain't got shit real, so you gotta come fuckin' wit' me." He laughed again. "What did you think I was gon' crack cuza all that shit y'all said? Did you think that I would confess? Man, I don't have shit to confess to." He made air quotes, mocking Detective Douglass. "Life in prison instead of the needle." He clapped; the sound like a firecracker. "That shit was priceless. But see, I ain't gotta cut no deals, cuz I ain't do shit."

He held out his hands as if waiting to be cuffed, just as he had the first time they questioned him. "Like I said one time before, unless y'all feel like y'all have enough to justify arrestin' me- I need to git back to work."

"We could charge you with obstruction of justice for not giving us the girlfriend's name," Douglass said.

Brock laughed again, continuing to hold his hands out. "Go hid, if you think that'll help you solve your case."

They let him go on his way, admiring his fortitude. He had become as hard as nails in record time. A brief stammer was the strongest reaction they'd gotten from replaying his crimes for him. This guy was not going to trip himself up.

"It's late, Mike," Dunbar said as he climbed into the driver's seat of the sedan. "I gotta drop you off and get back to my family. Not that I'll get a hero's welcome or anything."

"Yeah," Douglass agreed settling into the passenger seat. "My wife won't be too happy about me spending most of a Saturday working a case, either."

"There's no way we should try to pull this shit next weekend. Don't want to develop that habit at such a late date. Not if we don't wanna end up like all those cops with no family to go home to."

Douglass nodded his agreement as his partner entered traffic. "Are you kidding me? Without my family, this job wouldn't even be worth it. Not even with the pleasure of putting guys like that away."

"Oh, it will be a pleasure to put that guy away. But it won't happen unless we can break his cousin."

"Don't worry. I'll call Brunanski after Stephanie's done with my tongue lashing. That workaholic won't mind seeking out Terrell's mother and his girlfriend tomorrow while we're doing the family thing. See if we can get the ball rolling on him coming back to Baltimore sooner than he intended. I think he'll spill it all if we put enough pressure on him."

Dunbar nodded. "We'll find out soon enough if you're right about that," he said. "We'll find out soon enough."

IV

Brock realized that killing Mr. Johnson was the stupidest thing he'd done since the whole terrible mess began. He now doubted that the poor guy had seen Tia that night. If he had, it wouldn't have taken him so long to connect the dots with the girls' faces all over the news as they had been. Those cops had nothing until Brock went and stirred them up again.

*What the fuck got into me?* He wondered, deciding that he must have been out of his fucking mind.

He concluded that the drinking was what had pushed him over the edge. The drinking had made him paranoid, had made him think like a fool. Ever since the situation at Terrell's apartment happened, he was almost always drunk when he wasn't at work. He supposed he was becoming a real alcoholic, but given the choice between drowning in a bottle and drowning in his haunted thoughts, he'd choose the bottle every time.

Brock took another sip from the Bacardi bottle in his right hand, sitting at the foot of his bed in his unlit room. Jay-Z's distinct voice escaped the low volume of his combination alarm clock/radio, rapping about H to the IZZ-O, V to the IZZ-A. The burning liquid glided down Brock's esophagus, warming first his chest, then his belly. He took two more sips before he felt calm enough to consider the circumstances he now had to contend with.

His last conversation with those salt and pepper cops left no doubt that they had figured out everything that happened. Only the knowledge that it didn't matter if they had figured it out or not had kept Brock from cracking. What they could prove was what mattered and they had no physical evidence or witnesses to use against him. Shit, he'd be shocked if they could even get a search warrant. Even if some miracle resulted in them getting one, they wouldn't find anything to justify his arrest. After cleaning his car himself, he'd gone the extra mile of having it professionally detailed. They wouldn't find any evidence there and Terrell's apartment had been sanitized as well. Anyway, he seriously doubted any judge would sign off on a search warrant of college boy's apartment.

Brock took another sip of the rum. All of the weapons that had been used were in the Patapsco River and he'd burned the towels he used to muffle the gunshots. *Yeah, those cops got nothin' on me*, he thought, loosing a dry chuckle. *If they did, I'd be at Central Bookings instead of sittin' here alone in my room.*

Brock smirked, thinking of how deflated the detectives became after their best efforts didn't come close to cracking him. What did they think? That he would confess? Ha! There was no way in hell he'd ever fold under pressure.

Terrell was his biggest concern, not those detectives. Brock was sure that Terrell had gone to New York to stay with his roommate. There was nowhere else that he could've gone to chill out. He probably felt like he had to get away for a minute after what had happened to Tae. Brock could understand that, although Terrell's choice had put the cops on their trail even harder. He knew that Terrell would have to come back sooner or later.

When he did, the cops would put the full-court press on him, promising to go easy in exchange for cooperating against Brock. Brock wished that he could feel confident about how Terrell would hold up under such pressure, but the fact was that the dude was unstable. *Look at how he went off on me in the park,* Brock thought. *Tae would still be here if not for him.*

Brock wished he could talk to Terrell to figure out what was going on in his mind. But Terrell didn't have a cell phone and Brock didn't have any number for his roommate.

Still, Brock had to find a way to contact Terrell. He needed to know where Terrell's head was at. Only then would he know how to deal with his most beloved cousin.

V

A raven-haired Puerto Rican beauty chattered away as she sat next to Terrell. Her full figure held more curves than the Daytona Speedway. Her mountainous breasts heaved whenever she laughed or became otherwise animated. Pouty lips formed into a cupie doll smile as her piercing, hawk-like eyes regarded him.

Malik had met the raven haired girl's roommate (a petite beauty named Angela) a week or so before Terrell came up to visit him. He'd called her earlier that day to see what she meant to do tonight. She told him that she planned to go to the movies and bar hopping with her roommate. Ever the smooth talker, Malik had arranged a double date.

Terrell hadn't wanted to bother with any girls, but even he found it difficult to resist Malik's powers of persuasion. *Besides*, he thought, *I need something to keep my mind occupied.*

So Terrell had done his part for his friend, making conversation and buying drinks for the roommate. There was no need for her to know that he was spending Malik's money. One bad movie, three bars and a cab ride later, they all found themselves at the girls' apartment. It wasn't long before Malik and Angela departed for Angela's bedroom.

Terrell felt certain that the striking young woman before him had similar intentions, but he just wanted another drink. "Sorry to interrupt you," he lied, not having absorbed anything she'd said in the last two minutes, "but you got any liquor in here?"

"Sure thing, Papi," she said, giggling in her throaty Nuyorican accent. "How about a rum and coke?"

"Slow down, Papi," she said, her eyes bulging as he gulped the drink she handed him. "You'll put yourself out of it. Then you will be of no use to me."

Terrell giggled, the alcohol he had consumed so far that evening sneaking up on him. "Don't worry about me, Elizabeth," he said. "I kin hold my liquor."

"Dios Mi, Papi. It's *Elisabeth.* Not Elizabeth. I told you that earlier." She rolled her eyes. "Es mas bonita."

"I'm sorry," Terrell said, smiling. "Elisabeth. That is a lot prettier than Elizabeth. A pretty name for a pretty girl."

She blushed. "You think I'm pretty?"

"I think you're beautiful."

It was a bold-faced lie. Terrell didn't think she was beautiful. Fucking Hallie Berry was beautiful. Shit, Jennifer Lopez was beautiful. Fucking sexy was what Elisabeth was- sexy in the pornographic sense. She had a body that belonged on a Hot Latina Love x-rated DVD for sure. *Plus, I've never fucked a Puerto Rican,* Terrell thought. *I might as well hit it if I can. I don't have anything else better to do other than feel sorry for myself.*

Terrell patted his side pocket to make sure the condom Malik had given him was still there. No sooner had he done that than Elisabeth pounced on him, showing off numerous tricks of her pleasurable trade. Her pleasant fragrance, the feel of her long black hair, her gorgeous lips, voluptuous body, beautiful breasts, striking eyes, and expert hands all conspired to bring Terrell to ecstasy.

Elisabeth joined Terrell in sleep after they were done. All was quiet until he sprang from his perch in the middle of the night. His forceful movement knocked her off of him, into the small table in front of the couch.

"Fuck!" she screamed, her naked breasts jiggling. "You fucking asshole! What the fuck are you doing?"

Terrell felt too disoriented to answer, not yet realizing that the scene he'd just imagined was a nightmare.

"You trying to kill me, man?" Fury colored Elisabeth's hawk's eyes as she held her pained back. "Tu loco?"

Malik and Angela rushed from the bedroom, not knowing that doing so made things worse. Terrell had dreamed of the night when the girls were murdered. In his disorientation, he mistook the petite Angela for one of the Jenkins sisters.

"I won't let them hurt you," he said, running across the room to embrace her in an attempt at protection. He didn't notice Angela's screams anymore than he noticed that he was still naked.

"Be still!" he said, holding her firm as she exerted a furious struggle. "I promise I won't let them hurt you. Not this time."

Terrell didn't register Malik keeping the bilingually cursing Elisabeth from coming after him with a knife by tackling her onto the couch. Malik held the enraged girl's arms, using his sinewy weight to pin down the rest of her naked body.

"What is this?" Elisabeth snarled at him. "What are you fucking guys doing? You in this together? You going to rape me?"

"No!" Malik bellowed before dropping his voice to a quiet calm. "I'll be glad to let you up. But you gotta promise not to try to hurt my friend."

"That piece of shit is trying to hurt my friend!"

"No, he's not." Malik's words came rapid fire. "He wouldn't do that. He's just disoriented or something. Give me a chance to snap him out of it and then we'll get out of here."

"Alright." Elisabeth nodded, ceasing her struggles. "Alright. But you better hurry or I'm going to call the police."

"Terrell!" Malik bellowed as Terrell continued to bear hug Angela. She whimpered like a sad puppy, begging Terrell to let her go.

"Terrell! Let Angela go. That is my friend, Angela This is her apartment. She's not in danger and you don't need to protect her. Let her go!"

A cloudy haze departed Terrell's eyes as he released Angela. He looked around the apartment. "What the hell was I doing?" he asked no one in particular.

Elisabeth hurled Terrell's clothes at him, along with a barrage of bilingual curses and threats. Malik ushered him out in a whirlwind of activity as Elisabeth sent a fresh stream of curses into the hall to see them off.

After they managed to return to his basement quarters without further incident, Malik demanded to know what had gotten into his friend. Terrell shrugged, sitting on the edge of the cot. "I had a flashback or somethin', man. The way I woke up- the way those girls looked. It was like I was reliving a past experience."

"What past experience?"

Terrell's need to unburden himself was far stronger than his ability to birth further deceit. He poured out every detail of the horrid events that had transpired.

Malik gasped. "Oh, my God," he said. "What are you going to do?"

Terrell fell silent, having no answer to the question.

VI

Detective Brunanski waited for someone to answer Mrs. Hawkins's door, knowing that she was home, because her car waited in the driveway. Another car graced the street in front of her house. As he waited, Brunanski reflected on his first visit to the scenic residence.

During that Friday night encounter, Brunanski told Mrs. Hawkins that Terrell's upstairs neighbor had been murdered and that the police were interviewing everyone who lived in his building. He assured her that her son wasn't a suspect. He said that he only wanted to know if Terrell had seen anyone suspicious in or near the apartment complex.

Mrs. Hawkins told the detective that Terrell had gone to visit his college roommate in New York. He did not have a cell phone and had not left a contact number.

"My son is a big boy," she said. "It's not like he'll get into any trouble while he's there. You'll just have to talk to him when he gets back. It's not like he can stay away too long. The boy's got two jobs and rent to pay."

Brunanski had left his card, asking her to call when she heard from Terrell. She acted polite enough when she accepted it, but did not seem inclined to grant his request. He knew that she was suspicious of him because he was a cop, although she had no need to be at the time. He hadn't run into Douglass and Dunbar yet, hadn't learned about Terrell's possible connection to the Lake Montebello murders and Shawntae Kennard's disappearance.

Now that he was aware of those things, Brunanski felt much more determined to get something out of Mrs. Hawkins. He didn't think that she would spill the contact information even if she had it, but that was not what he had come for.

"Back again, detective?" Mrs. Hawkins said, eyeing him as she opened the inside door. She left the screen door closed. "And on a Sunday afternoon? I haven't heard from my son yet."

Brunanski nodded. "I figured as much. I've come here to find out if you're familiar with Terrell's girlfriend."

"Of course I am. My son wouldn't have a serious relationship with a young woman without introducing her to me. Monet's a sweet young lady."

"Well, do you think that she might be able to contact Terrell in New York? There's been a new development that makes contacting him very urgent."

Mrs. Hawkins's furrowed her brow. "What new development?"

Brunanski wagged a finger. "Uh-uh. You want to know something from me, Mrs. Hawkins - you have to help me out first. Now can you put me in touch with his girlfriend?"

Mrs. Hawkins frowned. "I suppose I can do that." She turned her back and yelled "Monet!" into the recesses of the house. "Come to the door."

A lovely young lady did just that. Mrs. Hawkins stepped aside, telling her that the detective had come looking for her.

"I'm Terrell's girlfriend," Monet said, speaking through the screen door as Mrs. Hawkins stood just behind her. "What can I do for you, detective?"

Brunanski scanned her lithe but curvy frame, flawless chestnut skin and striking ebony eyes, musing that he could think of a million things he'd like her to do for him. Alas, he had to maintain his professionalism. "Well, Miss..?"

"Monet. Monet Sanders."

"Yes, Miss Sanders. I understand that your boyfriend has gone to New York to visit a friend. I would just like to know if you have any idea when he's coming back or if you have any contact information for him. I'm investigating his upstairs neighbor's murder and I really need to talk to him."

The young beauty shook her head. "Poor Mr. Johnson," she said. Mrs. Hawkins placed a supportive hand on her shoulder. "He was a very nice man. He helped Terrell change a flat on my car once. Terrell isn't good at that sort of thing. We saw his body all covered up in front of Terrell's building the night it happened. We had just come back from the movies. It really shook Terrell up when we found out who it was. I think that's the main reason he went to New York, to clear his head. He hadn't planned on going until later this summer."

Brunanski nodded. "I imagine it must have been terrible for him to find out someone had been killed in front of his building, let alone someone he knew. Had Terrell been acting strange- maybe tense or jumpy prior to that?"

"No, not at all."

Brunanski felt that her answer had come too quickly and with too much certainty. This girl definitely knew something.

"Do you ladies mind if I come in? I'd hate to have to discuss such matters through your screen door."

Monet turned to Mrs. Hawkins, who nodded her assent. The young woman pushed the screen door open, giving Brunanski a wide berth as he entered. Years as a detective had acclimated him to being a source of suspicion and discomfort among ordinary citizens, whether they were hiding something or not. By his count, the percentage of those who were hiding something was nothing to sneeze at.

After settling onto the love seat across from the couch in Mrs. Hawkins's living room, Brunanski increased the intensity of his questioning.

"So, Miss Sanders. Do you have any contact information for Terrell in New York?"

Monet shook her head. "He hasn't called me yet. He's probably having too much fun. I expect him to call today, though." She laughed, exposing pearly white teeth. "If he doesn't, I'll get really mad."

Brunanski thought her laugh reeked of bullshit, as did her answer. No woman, young or old would let her boyfriend leave for an up all-night town like New York City without providing any contact information. "And you're certain that he hadn't been acting strange or jumpy- even before finding out about his neighbor?"

"Absolutely not," she said. Again, her response came much too quickly. An unsuspicious response would have been taking a moment to think before answering or even bristling at the question.

Mrs. Hawkins bristled on the couch that she shared with Monet. "Why do you keep asking her that? What reason does my son have to act strange?"

Brunanski didn't answer at first, instead looking from Mrs. Hawkins to Monet. He decided that the girlfriend knew what was going on and the mother didn't.

"None that I know of," he answered, leaning forward. "It's just that from a cynical perspective Terrell running off to New York right after his upstairs neighbor gets killed might make it appear that he knows something about it. From an even more cynical perspective, Terrell running off to New York might make it seem as if he had something to do with it."

"How dare you," Mrs. Hawkins hissed.

"I'm not speaking for myself, Ma'am. I'm just saying what it might look like from a cynical perspective. Terrell has a close friend named Shawntae Kennard- does he not?"

Mrs. Hawkins nodded. "Yes. Terrell and Tae have been close friends since he was in second grade. They and his cousin Damon are practically the three musketeers. What does that have to do…?"

"Shawntae Kennard has been missing since Thursday night. His mother filed the report. I thought you might have known."

Mrs. Hawkins's shocked facial expression struck the detective as genuine. Monet made a very credible attempt at seeming surprised, but the open mouthed gasp, confused eyes, and hands held to her perky chest all seemed contrived to Brunanski.

"Why would I have known that?" Mrs. Hawkins said, the shock on her face shifting into a scowl. "Shawntae is not my son. Terrell is. What are you implying?"

The detective ignored her and turned his attention to Monet. "You seem really shocked about this. Were you close with Mr. Kennard?"

"No!" Monet's voice grew shrill. "I only knew him through Terrell. But it's still terrible that he's gone missing."

Brunanski shrugged. "I couldn't agree with you more. To answer your earlier question, Mrs. Hawkins- I'm not implying anything. Implying isn't part of my job. I only examine the facts and the facts are that your son has taken off to New York at the exact same time that his upstairs neighbor was murdered and one of his best friends has gone missing."

He stared at Monet as if he were trying to see through her, causing her visible discomfort. "It will look awfully suspicious if he doesn't come back and talk to the police soon."

"I want you out of my house!" Mrs. Hawkins bellowed.

"Yes, Ma'am." Brunanski stood to leave, giving each of them one of his cards. "I'll be leaving now. But I need one or both of you to inform Terrell of the situation and have him call me as soon as you hear from him."

"Why should I have him call you?" Mrs. Hawkins fumed. "To help you try to pin something on him? My son is a decent young man." She pointed to the brown skin on her arm. "I know we all seem the same to you, but he is decent!"

"I'm sorry to upset you, Mrs. Hawkins," Brunanski said as he exited.

"Kiss my ass!" Mrs. Hawkins said, slamming the door behind him.

Brunanski sauntered away, feeling not the least bit offended, satisfied that he had done his part. He felt confident that the lovely Miss Sanders would soon do hers.

# Chapter Nine

I

Terrell affected a model of composure as he took Monet's panicked call on Malik's cell phone, urging her to calm down. She didn't need to know how close he felt to losing it himself. He assumed that the Detective who'd questioned her and his mom was in cahoots with Douglass and Dunbar. He figured that the three cops had pieced together everything that had happened, recognizing such as the best case scenario for him. The worse case scenario would be them concluding that he was responsible for it all. Terrell couldn't imagine any scenario in which the cops figured his hands were clean. The detectives couldn't yet prove whichever of the two scenarios they believed, but running off had made Terrell look guilty as sin. He had to return to Baltimore and talk to them. But what should he tell them?

A long prison term awaited him if he told the cops everything they needed to know. If he didn't tell them anything, he'd be left to his maniac cousin's mercy.

Terrell had no way of knowing if or when Brock might decide that he was a loose end that needed to be tied. Approaching the end game without a playbook terrified him.

He concluded his phone call with Monet by making a hollow promise that everything would be okay.

"How?" Her voice was an anguished moan. "How is it going to be okay?"

"It just will be." Terrell pressed the end button, wishing that he could believe his own assertion.

II

Sunday night found a somber Malik and Terrell standing at the Port Authority bus terminal, ignoring the dozens of other passengers waiting to be whisked off to myriad destinations.

"Sure you don't wanna stay?" Malik asked. "It's a lot calmer for you up here."

Terrell clasped his friend's hand. "'Preciate that. But I gotta face up to this. I can't be on the run forever."

"Some people do it."

Terrell nodded. "I know. But I can't live my life in fear. I gotta deal with the situation."

"But you don't even know how you're goin' to deal with the situation."

"I'll figure it out."

"Yeah? Well, you better do that real fast."

Terrell chuckled. "Believe me, I know that. Pray for me, man."

"You know I will," Malik said. "And I'm not even religious."

They both fell silent until Port Authority's loudspeaker announced the arrival of Terrell's bus. Malik extended his right hand, pulling Terrell into a rough half- hug.

"I hope to see you for fall classes, Baltimore."

"I hope to see you too."

"You be careful, son," Malik pleaded. "Be safe."

"I'll try," Terrell said. He turned and joined the line of people boarding his bus.

He would try to be safe. He would try to survive this ordeal with his life and his freedom intact. He knew the odds were long, but he would try.

III

Stark fear gripped Monet as she looked through the peephole.

She had never imagined Brock showing up on her doorstep, but there he was, a grim expression fixed on his face. Monet couldn't pretend to be elsewhere because her car sat out front.

At just past 9 p.m., it wasn't late enough to pretend to be asleep. *Besides*, Monet thought, *ducking him out will only confirm any suspicions he has about how much I know.* She wished her roommate was there, but Carletta was out with some new guy.

Monet considered the situation. Surely, Brock had not come to murder her. He had no reason to want to harm her at all. She calmed herself, concluding that he had come to ask about Terrell. Not knowing Terrell's whereabouts had to be driving him wild with fear. She would answer his questions, pretending ignorance for the most part and taking care not to let anything slip.

"Who is it?" she asked, after he knocked again.

"Iss Brock." His facial expression changed in a blink, matching the relaxed tone that he spoke in.

"Brock?"

"Yeah," he said, a sheepish smile blooming. "Sorry to drop in on you like this. I woulda called first, but I don't have your number."

"It's okay. Just give me a chance to throw something on." She rushed to her bedroom, replacing the tight cotton tank top and boy shorts she wore with a tee shirt and elastic sweatpants. She wrestled her visage into an illusion of pleasant surprise before opening the door. "What can I do for you?"

For the second time that day, that innocent question inspired filthy thoughts in a man. Brock thought that she looked damn fine, even in a tee shirt and sweats. It was all he could do to keep from leering.

"Sorry to pop in on you, baby girl," he said, showing no interest in stepping inside. "I was hopin' Terrell was around. I ain't heard from him in a couple days 'n' he hasn't been answerin' his phone."

Monet paused before answering, trying to gauge what the least suspicious response would be. She decided to give him some well filtered truth. "He didn't tell you he went to New York?"

Brock's eyes widened. "Naw," he said. "He didn't tell me no shit like that. What- is he up there wit' his roommate?"

"Malik." Monet nodded and smiled. "Yeah."

"So he went to New York 'n' he didn't tell nobody but you. Don't that seem strange?"

Monet shrugged. "I assumed he had told other people. But- he kind of has to tell his girlfriend, you know? You wouldn't go out of town without telling your girl anything. Would you?"

Brock frowned. "I don't keep girlfriends. So I don't know nothin' 'bout that. When did he leave?"

"Friday. I took him to the Travel Plaza."

"Was he actin' strange before he left?"

Monet chuckled. "Why would he be acting strange? I don't mean to be rude Brock- but you're asking an awful lot of questions. I'm starting to feel like I'm trapped in an episode of 'Law and Order' or something." She held out her right hand, palm facing up as if waiting for something to be placed in it. "May I see your badge, officer?"

A strange expression started to emerge on Brock's face, but a smile shoved it aside. He laughed, taking one step back from the doorway. "I'm sorry, girl. I guess I was comin' off a lil' bit like a cop."

Monet shrugged. "That's okay. I think its' sweet that you're worried because you haven't heard from him."

Brock frowned. "I don't know about it bein' sweet 'n' all," he said. "But like I said, I haven't heard from him in a while. What I'm really worried about is that Tae's missing. I thought Terrell might know somethin' about it."

"Tae's missing?"

Brock felt that it had taken a fraction of a second too long for surprise to register on Monet's face. She was faking. Terrell had told her something. He might have told her everything.

"Yeah. No one's seen him since Thursday night. I was hopin' Terrell had heard from him."

"He didn't say anything about Tae before he left." Her eyes widened. "I hope Tae's okay."

Brock nodded. "So do you know when Terrell's coming back?"

Monet shook her head. "No. I guess he's kind of playing it by ear."

"He calls you from there, though," Brock said, an impish smile spreading across his face. "I know I'd call home every day if I had a fine girl like you. Shit, I might not be able to leave in the first place."

"Thank you." The smile Monet's mouth formed disagreed with the look in her eyes. "He does call."

Brock stepped back from the porch. "Smart man. If he calls tonight, tell 'im he don't have to hurry back. Tell 'im I'll be happy to keep an eye on you while he's gone."

He winked at her, a threatening and obscene gesture coming from him. He turned and walked to his car, snickering as he did so. Monet stood stunned as he stopped in front of it, smiled and waved.

It took a colossal effort for her to smile and wave back, pretending ignorance aware of the true meaning of what he'd just said, pretending that she didn't feel more afraid than she had ever been in her life.

IV

Terrell arrived at the Travel Plaza just short of 2:30 a.m. He called Monet from a phone booth, ignoring the cast of unsavory characters who shared the station with him at that odd hour.

"Hello?"

"Damn, girl. You sound wide awake. What- did you go out tonight? I've neva known you for goin' out on Sundays."

Monet sounded beside herself as she rattled off the details of Brock's visit.

"That muthafucka," Terrell growled. The sight of a security guard deterred him from punching something. "That muthafucka. I can't believe he came at you like that."

He composed himself enough to tell Monet where he was.

V

"Where do you want to go?" Monet asked as Terrell climbed into her car. It had taken her less than half an hour to arrive at the Travel Plaza.

His response came after a pensive silence. "Let's go back to your place. Cops might come around to my place and I don't want them to know I'm back until I'm sure about what I want to say to them."

Monet merged onto 1-95 North a few moments later, exiting it on 6-95 and staying on that highway until reaching the Perring Parkway South exit. The cul-de-sac of townhouses that she lived in waited a few minutes away.

Terrell thought only of resting as he exited the car. He wanted a good, long sleep before emerging to play out the string of his disastrous ordeal.

"Yo, Terrell." An unmistakable and unwelcome voice permeated the darkness behind him. A terrified tremor coursed through his body as he turned to face his caller, realizing that he would have no rest at all.

VI

"Terrell!" Brock called a second time as he stepped from the darkness into the illumination provided by neighboring porch lights.

Monet gasped as Terrell's hands formed fists. "What the fuck are you doin' here, man?" Terrell barked.

Brock smiled, moving toward Terrell with his hands held palms out. "I wouldn't suggest you git all belligerent 'n' shit. Don't you know this is a nice neighborhood? You might disturb one baby girl's neighbors 'n' they might call the cops or somethin'. N' I know you don't wanna see no cops. Do you, cuz?"

"Why don't you leave him alone?" Monet's voice trembled as she glared at Brock.

"Why don't you leave us alone, sexy?" Brock's smile morphed into something leering and devilish. "Told you I'd be keepin' my eye on you. Tha's what I was doin'- waitin' in the shadows when you went drivin' off at 2 somethin' in the mornin'. That surprised me- but not as much as you returnin' wit' Baltimore's most wanted right here. I appreciate you makin' our reunion possible, though. Now, why don't you go on in the house? Me 'n' your boyfriend got a lot to talk about."

Monet glared at Brock and crossed her arms. "I'm not leaving him alone with you."

Brock cackled like a hyena, throwing his head back and slapping his right knee. "Oh, shit! So you really were dumb enough to tell her everything? Got damn, cuz. Why you do that?" He shrugged. "I guess you couldn't carry the weight on your own."

Brock turned out all his pockets and lifted his shirt, continuing to hold it up as he did a slow turn. His smile dissipated. "I don't have anything, baby," he said. "I jus' wanna talk. Me 'n' Terrell gotta work things out so we kin both git out of this situation wit' our asses 'n' our freedom."

"I don't believe a word you say," Monet hissed. "You're sick."

"Go on in, Mo." Terrell embraced her, kissing her forehead. "I'll be fine."

Monet's eyes pleaded for him to allow her to stay. "But…"

Terrell kissed her lips. "I'll be fine," he said. Monet said nothing more, kissing him back before doing as he asked.

"I won't be long, baby," Terrell promised as she looked through the screen door. "Go on 'n' lay down. I won't be long."

"Aw, that's so sweet," Brock mocked as Monet disappeared into the townhouse. "You know that girl really loves you, cuz? You should try not to put her through so much."

"Fuck you."

"Damn, cuz. Tha's how you feel? I hope not, cuz we got to come to one accord." Brock turned and began walking across the cul-de-sac. "Follow me."

"Follow you?" Terrell struggled to keep from yelling. "For all I know you might have a gun stashed around here."

Brock turned to face his cousin. "You really think that shootin' you would be in my best interest?"

"I guess not," Terrell answered after a long silence.

"Then come on, man." They left the cul-de-sac, turning left and coming to a block of well-kept, streetlight lit row houses. Brock's Cutlass Supreme sat parked in front of one of them.

"Couldn't very well park in your girl's lot," he said. "If I did that she mighta known I was watching."

"So you parked here 'n' hid out on foot so you could watch her?" Terrell said, ignoring his best instincts and climbing into the passenger seat. "Man, you're sick."

Brock shrugged. "Not sick. Jus' desperate. I watched her place from right here, seein' if anybody came or went, hopin' you'd show up. I was about to give up when I saw her leave that last time. Right away I figga'd she'd gone to pick you up. Jus' like I figga'd y'all would come back here. You were problee worried about me or the cops lookin' for you at your place." He tapped his right temple with his index finger. "Ever since this whole bullshit started, I've had to try to think two or three steps ahid- try to figga out what the fuck erybody else who's mixed up in this shit might do and respond accordingly. I'm smarter than the average bear, cousin. Smart enough to think about ery detail a this fuckin' shit."

"Either that or you've lost every one of your marbles."

Brock eyes widened for a moment before he relaxed into a smile that would have been pleasant in less hideous circumstances. "Iss easy for you to call me crazy, Terrell. If you kin convince yourself that I'm crazy, then you kin lie to yourself 'n' say you wouldn't do any of the shit I done if you were in my shoes." He paused, the smile twisting into a scowl. "But I'ma remind you that that's bullshit. You had a choice about killin' Tae. Didn't you?"

Terrell didn't answer.

"Yeah, I figga'd you wouldn't have nothin' to say about that. Jus' rememba, your hands are dirty now, too. You got one body, I got four. We both go down if we don't work togetha." He slapped the dashboard. "Do you understand that? Do you?"

"Yeah, man," Terrell said, looking straight ahead. "I understand."

Brock took a deep breath. "Good. Now you know them two detectives got this whole shit figga'd out- right? They know iss all connected. The girls, Tae disappearin', Mr. Johnson, 'n' you runnin' off like that. They let me know in so many words that they think I'm the main guy, which means they gon' lean on you soon as they know you're back. What they don't figga on is that you did Tae."

Though he kept looking straight ahead, Terrell felt the intensity of the unbroken stare that Brock cast upon him. "Maybe if you hadn't done Tae, you'd give me up," Brock growled. "Shit, maybe if you hadn't come at me all crazy Tae wouldn't a got hurt in the first place."

"Kiss my fuckin' ass with that maybe shit," Terrell hissed. "Shit is what it is. I don't need to listen to no fuckin' multiple murderer try to paint me as bein' bad as him." He turned and glared at Brock. "Just tell me how you think we should handle the cops."

# Chapter Ten

I

Terrell appreciated every moment of peace that passed on Monday, July 11, knowing that it was the calm before a raging storm. Being waited on hand and foot by Monet wasn't anything close to a bad deal. Neither were a few spirited romps in the sack. Terrell collapsed into a peaceful slumber after their third go round.

When Terrell awoke the next morning, he felt reinvigorated and ready to take on the whole world if he had to. He didn't have to take on the whole world, but he did have to take on two determined homicide detectives.

II

Detective Douglass faced Terrell from across the tiny interview room table. Detective Dunbar sat to his partner's right. Terrell had contacted them right after finishing the country breakfast Monet prepared, telling them that he was ready to answer their questions. He knew that they would try to break him inside this stuffy little room, but he didn't intend to be moved.

"There seems to be a whole shit storm of unfortunate events happening around you," Dunbar started in, leaning across the table so that Terrell could feel his warm breath. "Doesn't there?"

Terrell shrugged. "Shit happens all the time."

Dunbar smiled. "You're definitely right about that. Thing is- the same shit doesn't keep happening to the same people. Not unless they're mixed up in something."

"Nothing has happened to me. Things have happened around me, but nothing has happened to me."

"Really?" Douglass chimed in. He rose from his seat and stood beside Terrell. "So you don't consider your upstairs neighbor being brutally murdered and probably your best friend disappearing to have happened to you?"

Terrell shook his head. "No- I mean- of course I'm affected by that. I wish I knew where Tae was- and Mr. Johnson getting killed messed me up. That's why I went to New York a little earlier than I had planned. I'll probably move after my lease runs out. I can't feel comfortable coming home to a place where someone's been murdered."

"You have very good interview speech."

"What?"

Douglass smiled. "You know what I'm talking about. Us smart brothers have to be bilingual, right? The Queen's English and Ghettoese. I bet every other word is slang or mispronounced when you're 'hangin' wit' the boys'. 'You feel me'?"

"It's a good tactic," Dunbar said, following his partner's lead. "Right now you need to come off like Joe College, not some yo boy. Of course if you had chosen to be Joe College all the time, instead of 'slummin' witcha ghetto friends you might not have gotten mixed up in all this shit in the first place."

"I'm not mixed up in anything."

"Sure you are." Dunbar rose from his seat and stood to Terrell's left, leaving him boxed in. "You're mixed up in at least four murders, and I'll bet a broke leg horse at next year's Preakness your buddy Shawntae makes it five."

Terrell chuckled. "Man, you don't know what you're talkin' about."

Douglass plopped into the chair his partner had vacated, slapping the tabletop. "We don't know what we're 'talkin' about?" he mocked. "That's more how you talk around your buddies, right?"

"There you go again. What does it matter to you whether or not I pronounce the letter g?"

"It doesn't matter to me. But it matters an awful lot to you."

Douglass folded his arms and slouched back in his chair. "Hey, I've been there. I know how it is to be a smart guy hanging around guys who aren't so smart."

"Really?" Terrell frowned. "Who told you about it?"

Douglass clapped his hands as he laughed. "Touche'. Maybe I don't seem so smart to a bright young scholar like you, but there's plenty going on in this shiny noggin. Shit, I'm smart enough to have pieced together everything that's happened involving these murders."

Dunbar cleared his throat.

Douglass shot a glance at his squat colleague. "My bad, partner. I did have some help from the big man here and the esteemed Detective Brunanski- whom you've never had the pleasure of meeting. Yup, the three of us together were plenty smart enough to figure out how a smart guy like you got mixed up with all these bodies. Would you like to hear our theory?"

Terrell smiled, slouching in his seat as if settling in on his own couch. "Sure. Maybe after I refute whatever bullshit you have to say you'll leave me alone."

"Oh, but it's not bullshit," Douglass said, his smile broader than Terrell's. "This is primo stuff you're about to hear."

"Primo," Dunbar echoed.

Terrell smirked, motioning for the detective to proceed. The man's partner continued to stand closer than Terrell liked.

"As I was saying, I know how it is to be a smart guy with friends who aren't so bright. Sometimes you do things that you wouldn't do on your own - just to show them that you don't think you're better than them."

"Things like hooking up with some random sluts and having a sex party," Dunbar added, leaning over so that his words poured into Terrell's ear.

"You're absolutely right, partner!" Douglass jumped out of his seat. Sitting back down, he fixed a hard stare on Terrell. "That's what we think happened to you. I mean- a smart and beautiful girl like the one you go around with? You mess around on her with some skanks you picked up off the corner? It had to be peer pressure. Don't you think, partner?"

Dunbar smiled as he nodded, resting a chubby hand on Terrell's shoulder. "Had to be."

Terrell scooted his seat to the right to free himself of Dunbar's hand. He felt beads of sweat emerging on his forehead. "You guys enjoy this part of your job-don't you?"

"Beats flipping burgers," The robust detective said. "What's a matter? You getting nervous? Heard something too close to home? "

"I'm not worried. Regardless of whatever fantasy scenario you guys have concocted, I'm innocent."

"Concocted!" Douglass pounded a dark fist on the table. "That's a high rent word if I ever heard one. Bet you never break that one out around Tweedle Dee and Tweedle Dum."

"Who says my friends are dumb?"

"Not who. What. Their educational record."

"Whatever. You going to finish that shit you were talkin'? I don't have all day."

"Sorry. It's just so much fun 'talkin' with you. But I digress. So we figure at this little sex party you have, you all get just as drunk as a school of fish."

"Don't forget about the marijuana," Dunbar added.

"Thanks, big guy! There was marijuana in those girls' systems." Douglass slapped himself upside the head. "How could I forget that? Maybe I'm not so smart after all. Anyway, with all those substances being consumed, we figure something got out of hand, maybe some rough play or something."

"I don't see how their systems could be tested for anything," Terrell countered. "According to the news, their remains were in a bad state after being pulled from the water."

Detective Douglass chuckled, winking at Terrell. "Watch a lot of news, do you?"

"I try to stay informed."

"Well, the News was right. Their bodies were pretty far gone. But you'd be surprised at the miracles that can be performed with modern blood work."

"I wouldn't be surprised if a cop lied about something like that, though," Terrell said, sneering.

Douglass ignored Terrell's assertion, looking to Detective Dunbar and asking a question that Terrell knew he already knew the answer to. "What's the name of the victim who died from a head wound?"

"Tia Jenkins."

"Yeah, that's right." Douglass looked back to Terrell. "We figure poor Tia hit her head really hard, probably died by accident."

Terrell gulped, trying not to replay that night in his head. He couldn't help being affected by the memories the detectives' tactics stirred up.

Douglass continued. "After that -shit - after that- things got way out of hand." He fell silent for a few moments, adopting a conspiratorial tone when he spoke again. "You know no one would blame you for what happened, right?"

Terrell shrugged. "Nothing happened around me."

"Sure it did. A girl had an unfortunate accident. One that proved fatal. Maybe that was something that could have been cleared up without you guys getting into too much trouble, but you were all so scared. Of the three of you, your cousin Brock was probably the one dead set against calling the authorities and cutting your losses. He's the one who probably killed the poor girl and he didn't like his chances if he fessed up - what with having a violent offense already on his record."

"You guys are trying to figure out what you're gonna do when one of the other girls or maybe both of them flip out," Dunbar chimed in. "Before you guys know it you have to subdue them."

More perspiration beaded Terrell's forehead as his arms birthed a litter of goose bumps.

Douglass smiled at his partner. "I thought I was telling this."

"I'm sorry, partner. I just got way into that shit."

Douglass chuckled. "That's because I'm such an eloquent storyteller," he chuckled. He pointed at Terrell. "You wanna help- get this guy some water. He's pouring sweat. The room must be too hot for him."

"I would, but I don't want to miss any of your fantastic storytelling."

"I don't need any damn water!" Terrell bellowed, banging on the table. "Go on and finish what you have to say."

Douglass smiled. "Sure thing. Anyway, Brock's will wins out and you all end up doing the other two." He shook his head. "Nah, that doesn't play right. *He* ends up doing the other two. You and Shawntae were just too overwhelmed to stop him. Who could blame you? You know? How could a person ever prepare themselves to deal with that situation? They don't teach a class on it in school."

As the detective laughed, Terrell realized that he was doing more than just relating a theory. He was giving Terrell a chance to lie about Brock and make things easier for himself. The cops were in terrible need of a scapegoat and Terrell was their chosen tool to snag Brock as such. Their confidence in getting Terrell to say what they wanted him to say bordered on arrogance. Terrell boiled inside as he grew even more determined to stand them off.

"So anyway, you felt terrible about what happened. But the guy's still like a brother to you – right? You're all like brothers. So you help him get rid of the bodies. It took some stern stuff to chop them up like that. I don't know if I could've done it - but then I've never been in the situation. Walk a mile in a man's shoes and all that good shit. You know?"

Dredged up memories stung Terrell like a hive of angry wasps. He considered stopping the exchange, asking for a lawyer. But he didn't want to leave without convincing the detectives that he couldn't be broken. He steeled himself for more of their mind games.

"So you guys get rid of the bodies and go back to life as usual," Douglass continued. "You try not to think about the shit that happened and you never mention it. But then, the bodies get discovered so you all come up with an alibi. It's a good alibi, too- especially considering the girls' reputations. Shit, it would have been impossible for us to mark you guys as solid suspects if one of you hadn't panicked and killed Mr. Johnson. Do you know we weren't even the primaries on that one?"

Terrell examined Detective Douglass's pleased as pie smile, musing that it was very possible that the man had a hard on.

"No sir, our buddy Detective Thomas Brunanski caught that one," the detective said. "Ole Mr. Solo Flight himself. We happened to run into him at our favorite greasy spoon. Over in Hampden, Hon. A little shop talk and the next thing you know we're playing connect the murders. Not that we think you killed anybody. You're not the type. So why don't you make it easier on everyone and tell us all about what your cousin Damon did? Then this will finally be over. I know it has to be tearing you up inside."

"You'll get a lot less jail time if you cooperate," Dunbar added, leaning over and treating Terrell to more of his warm breath.

Terrell scowled. "I'm not doing any jail time, because I didn't do anything," he said. "And I don't know what the hell y'all mean about telling you what Brock did."

"You didn't do anything?" Dunbar said. He snatched Terrell out of his seat, shoved him into the wall behind the table and pinned him against it. "Last time I checked being an accessory to a triple murder is a huge deal. So is obstruction of justice!"

"I'm not obstructing anything."

"Then just what the fuck do you call knowing who gunned down your neighbor in cold blood and not doing shit about it? What the fuck do you call it when you won't tell what you know about your missing friend?"

"Git the fuck off me!" Terrell screeched, struggling to get free.

"I'm not on you yet, you little shit!" Dunbar said, forcing Terrell back against the wall.

"Alright, let him go!" Douglass pulled his partner away and placed himself between the two combatants. "Take a walk, big man."

Terrell smirked, straightening his ruffled shirt after Dunbar left the room. "What was that? I'm supposed to believe you stopped him from kickin' my ass? I guess that makes you the good cop, huh?"

"No. I'm just a cop, period," Douglass answered. He sat back down, motioning for Terrell to join him. "He really was about to kick your ass. My partner's passionate that way."

"Yeah?" Terrell settled in, keeping his eyes alert. "Well if he had kicked my ass, I would've sued the police department passionately."

"Oh, I don't doubt that. But that wouldn't have helped you heal from the beating he would have given you any quicker."

Terrell shrugged. "Look, man- I don't know what y'all want from me. I don't know anything about any murders or Brock doing anything. I sure don't know where the hell Tae is. If I was involved in anything, why would I talk to y'all voluntarily? I don't have to be here."

Douglass nodded. "You're right. You don't have to be here. You're not under arrest. And you can go on lying about not knowing anything about where your friend Shawntae is. But how do you explain being the last person he spoke to on his cell phone? Isn't that one coincidence too many?"

Terrell almost panicked at that revelation, but then he remembered that Tae had to have called Brock for a ride to the park, because they were together when Terrell arrived. This lying cop would say whatever was necessary to get Terrell to spill the beans. It was time to make him realize that would never happen.

"First of all, why should I believe that I was the last person to talk to Tae?" Terrell said. "Because you said so? Yeah, I'm sure you're gonna be completely honest with me, cop. Tell you what-I'm tired of this shit, man. Y'all cops tryna say I'm involved in all this shit? Do y'all have a murder weapon? DNA? Witnesses? Shit, you obviously can't even justify gittin' a search warrant for my apartment, but I'm supposed to admit to some bullshit? What –y'all thought y'all could intimidate me?" He sneered as he rose from his seat. "I tell you what, Detective Douglass. Until y'all have enough to actually charge me with somethin', y'all kin kiss my ass." He chuckled. "So I guess you'll be puckering up for the foreseeable future."

Detective Douglass sat speechless, his jaw collapsing toward the floor. Terrell saw hope depart from his adversary's eyes. They had been so sure they could break him. Maybe they could have broken the person he was before all of this began. But there was no breaking the person he had become.

"We can get a search warrant," Douglass protested, sounding as if he lacked belief in his own words.

Terrell shrugged. "Get it, if you really can. Even if you do, you won't find anything."

"And if we don't, the person who's killed all these people gets away with it?" Detective Douglass sounded wounded.

"I think that everyone pays for what they've done, sooner or later."

Realizing that no response was forthcoming, Terrell asked if he was free to go.

Too despondent to speak, the detective waved Terrell away. His partner blocked Terrell's path as Terrell left the interview room and started toward the police station exit. Terrell made unflinching eye contact with the heavy set man.

"Your partner just dismissed me. Apparently, he doesn't think you guys have enough to justify arresting me or holding me."

Dunbar's Adam's apple bobbled as he swallowed hard. "I guess it's your lucky day, then. But I wouldn't leave town if I were you."

Terrell shrugged. "Why would I leave town? I just got back."

He stood outside of the police station moments later, having decided that his next course of action depended on whether or not the cops managed to get a search warrant for his apartment and what such a search warrant turned up. If they searched the place and found traces of any of those girls' blood, he'd sing like a canary and hope for the best deal possible. Otherwise, he'd carry the dreadful secrets of all that had happened to his grave. He just hoped that Brock wouldn't decide to send him to that grave early.

# Epilogue

A knapsack clad Terrell found Brock waiting outside his apartment building on a balmy September morning. He froze in his tracks, standing silent as his cousin looked him over.

"Your eyes are 'bout as bloodshot as mine," Brock said.

Terrell shrugged. "I keep having bad dreams. Bad memories."

Brock forced a smile onto his gaunt and haggard face. His diminished frame now swam in clothes that were once merely baggy. "I feel you on 'at, cuz. Me-I don't even fall asleep regula' no more. I got to pass out from drunkness."

Terrell furrowed his brow as his voice dropped into a furious whisper. "I'm supposed to give a fuck?"

Brock chuckled. "Oh…so you still on 'at shit? No love for the bad guy. Right?"

"What the fuck do you want?"

"I jus' wanted to see how you doin'. We ain't really talked since that thing wit' the cops."

Detectives Douglass and Dunbar had obtained a search warrant for Terrell's apartment the day after they interrogated him. A Forensics team scoured the place for trace DNA, but they couldn't find anything that placed any of the three dead girls there. Not privy to the exact science of forensics, Terrell guessed that the thorough cleaning that had been done on numerous occasions had conspired with the passage of time to eliminate any useful traces. The results of the search pretty much killed any case the cops hoped to build. Brock and Terrell's last encounter had been a meeting to discuss the fortuitous results.

"I don't want to talk to you, Brock. And I'm obviously never going to tell anyone anything about what happened. We're both still walking free. Aren't we?"

Brock shook his head. "Free from jail, but…"

"But what, man? I'm not going to stand here and listen to you talk about feeling guilty. I got my own shit to deal with."

"You're talkin' different," Brock said.

"Don't worry about how the fuck I talk."

Brock held his hands out in a gesture of surrender. "Listen, cuz. I know you hate my guts. You should, too. But I jus' wanna talk to you about things one good time. If I don't talk to you- I'll neva git to talk about it at all. Just one time, cuz. After that, I swear I'll neva bother you again."

Terrell stroked his now scruffy goatee as he considered Brock's plea. "You swear?"

Brock made the sign of the cross over his heart. "I swear."

"Alright, Brock. But not out here." He turned and walked inside.

Terrell removed his knapsack from his shoulders settled onto his loveseat a few moments later, leaving Brock the couch.

"Where's your roommate, cuz?"

"He had an eight o'clock class. I'm on my way to class myself - so make it quick."

"Alright, cuz. Iss jus that…I don't think I'll eva be right. You know?"

Terrell unleashed a bitter laugh. "Of course I know. I'll never be right, either. Thanks to you."

"There you go wit' that bullshit again, cuz. You made your own choices."

Terrell exploded to his feet. "My own choices? Fuck you, Brock! You kin git out - you murderous muthafucka! I ain't goin' down this road witchu!"

"No. I'm sorry, Terrell. I'm sorry," Brock whimpered. "I won't say no more shit like that. I swear. Please jus' hear me out, cuz."

Veins pulsed in Terrell's forehead and neck as he looked at his watch. "Make it fast." He plopped back down, poised at the edge of his seat.

Brock sat silent for a few moments before speaking.

"Basically, man…even though we got away wit' the shit…. We didn't. I ain't neva' gon be right, cuz. I'm carryin' around all this fuckin' guilt….but the only way to git rid a it is to confess to the stupid ass cops. I do that, I die. Iss lethal injection for sure. 'N' I don't wanna die. Miserable as I am… I don't wanna die."

Terrell realized that Brock was trembling. He possessed a perfect understanding of his cousin's sentiments. He might even have felt sorry for Brock, if he didn't find him so revolting.

Brock's lips quivered as tears welled in his eyes. "I think I'm becomin' an alcoholic. I'm drinkin' more than ever jus' to git through the day. Drinkin' even more jus' to git to sleep."

He wiped his tears, taking several deep breaths. A wan smile crept onto his face as he regained his composure. "You know, I really thought you were gon' cave to the cops. While I was worried about what you said to them, I almost regretted not killin' you. Kin you believe that shit, cuz?"

Terrell shrugged. "I believe you're capable of anything."

Brock gasped and clutched his abdomen. "I know. I know. 'N' tha's so fucked up, man. How did I git to be a fuckin' monster? The shit I've done, cuz. The shit I made you do." He stood up and began pacing. Tears slid down his face. "You know Miss Kennard is sick now? She's problee gon' die now….die from sadness. That shit is cuz a me. Cuz a me, she won't even git to give her son a funeral, even though she got to know he's dead. Because of me, lil David gon' grow up wit' no fava. Because of me, a couple families been destroyed."

Brock smacked his left palm. "You know at the time that I did everything I did, I was jus' tryna survive, cuz. But now that it seems like we're in the clear…. I can't stop thinkin' about how terrible it all was. I acted like a monster, Terrell. I am a monster."

Terrell nodded. "Yes, you are."

"I know I am!" Brock yelped, wiping his face again. "'N' the worse thing about it is, no matta' how terrible I feel -even though I got stomach problems 'n' erything- I know that I could neva turn myself in."

Terrell sighed, pressing a thumb against his chest. "I got to carry my guilt around for the rest of my days, too. I'm not as bad as you, but I'm far from a saint."

"How you gon' do it?"

Terrell shrugged. “I don’t know, man. I’ll start by getting out of Baltimore. I’m transferring to a college down south next semester. Just being here is horrible. Being in this apartment is worst of all.”

“I feel you. What about your girl, though?”

Terrell shook his head. “I don’t have a girl, anymore.”

Brock’s eyes widened. “You broke up wit’ shorty?”

“She deserves better than to be mixed up with some fucked up dude like me.”

Brock nodded. An idea streaked through his mind, causing his eyes to grow even wider. “You think she’ll eva tell anybody?”

Terrell sprang upon Brock, grabbing him and driving him into the couch. His eyes blazed with ferocity as he wrapped his hands around Brock’s scrawny neck. “If you even think about touching her- I'll kill you! Do you understand that? I will kill you!”

The realization that Brock hadn't bothered to struggle stilled Terrell’s volcanic fury. He rolled off his cousin, placing his hands to his own temples.

Brock coughed and hacked as he straightened up, rubbing his throat until the pained noises ebbed away.

“I wouldn’t even a cared if you’d done it, cuz.” His voice sounded strained when he managed to speak. “Shit, I don't know. Maybe I wouldn't mind dyin’ so much. Only I wouldn’t want you to throw your life away on me.”

“Too late for that,” Terrell said. He retreated to the loveseat, rubbing his hands on his clothes in disgust. “My life hasn't been shit since I let you do what you did.”

“You're right, cuz,” Brock rasped. “I guess neitha a us is eva gon’ be right again.”

# Also by T.R. Braxton:

## *Sight*

Young Nathan Walker performs feats with his mind that normal humans can't fathom, feats that drain his mind and body. His ability is vital in keeping his father, James, an early twentieth century civil rights activist, from harm at the hands of rural Alabama racists. The family flees to Baltimore, where James establishes himself as a successful businessman and prominent member of the fledgling NAACP. While Nathan struggles with his burgeoning talents and a much larger new school, James's relentless activism pushes him ever closer to danger. Tragedy strikes when Nathan's fear of his own power causes him to turn away from it. In the wake of that tragedy, Nathan focuses his vast and frightening capabilities on revenge. He will not stop until vengeance is his, even if he must sacrifice himself to obtain it.

*Available at trbraxton.com and wherever books and e-books are sold.*

www.ingramcontent.com/pod-product-compliance
Lightning Source LLC
LaVergne TN
LVHW010613100826
845148LV00014B/2947
* 9 7 8 0 9 8 4 1 2 4 4 0 4 *